Copyright © 2024 by Theophilus Monroe.

All rights reserved. Printed in the United States of America. No part of this book may be used or reproduced in any manner whatsoever without written permission except in the case of brief quotations embodied in critical articles or reviews.

Cover Design by Deranged Doctor Design

Proofreading/Editing by Mel: https://getproofreader.co.uk/

This book is a work of fiction. Names, characters, businesses, organizations, places, events and incidents either are the product of the author's imagination or are used fictitiously. Any resemblance to actual persons, living or dead, events, or locales is entirely coincidental.

For information:

www.theophilusmonroe.com

THE FURY OF A VAMPIRE WITCH
BOOK 8

BLOODY MOON

THEOPHILUS MONROE

Chapter 1

THE THROBBING BASS POUNDED in my ears like a second heartbeat as I slid through the sweaty mass of human bodies. The club reeked of spilled alcohol, cheap perfume, and the tang of fresh blood. I wrinkled my nose in disgust.

Not at the blood smell. That was delectable. But the damn perfume. What were the kids wearing these days, anyway? Eau de Dog Shit? It was *almost* as bad as that damn body spray the young men used to wear. I was glad when that crap fell out of fashion.

"Come on, Mercy!" Juliet grabbed my wrist, dragging me onto the dance floor. "Loosen up a little."

I scowled, glancing back at Mel and Muggs waiting by the bar. "You know this isn't my scene. I don't go 'clubbing' for fun. I go to places like this to *eat*."

Juliet laughed, tossing her pink hair. "We all agreed. No biting *anyone* tonight. This is about enjoying ourselves for once. When's the last time we actually got to have some fun? No missions, no dragons trying to un-make the world, no pissed off djinn. Just relax, girl."

I released a deep breath and surveyed the crowd. Not a person there who was a day over thirty. Children, really, compared to us. Mel was the only one of our bunch who wasn't far removed from *this* generation's kind of fun.

Back in my day, dance was an *art*. You took lessons. You practiced. We were *graceful*.

These days, though? Shake your body to the beat, pretend you're having a seizure, and you could call it dancing. Half the people out on the dance floor looked certifiable. Dance like that when I was growing up, and they'd lock you up for sure.

Juliet held out her hand. "You coming? Or are you going to stand there swaying back and forth like an awkward kid at a middle school dance?"

"Never been to one of those. We didn't have school 'dances' in my time. I wouldn't know. How would you?"

Juliet rolled her eyes. "Television. Movies. Whatever. You're stalling."

"Mercy!" Mel shouted, bobbing her way over to us. She grabbed my hand. "Pull that stake from your arse and get out here!"

"I *don't* have a *stake* up my—"

"Could have fooled me," Juliet interrupted with a smirk.

I glanced over at Muggs. He wasn't having any fun, either. I mean, who would have thought that bringing a blind druid who actually *looked* his ancient age was a good idea? Juliet and Mel, that's who. "Maybe I'll just go sit with Muggs. He's clearly out of his element."

"Stop being such an old fart!" Mel shouted.

"I might be old, but I'm not a goddamn fart, Mel!" I screamed back, frustrated not as much by Mel's comment as the fact I had to raise my voice to be heard at all. That's the worst part about clubs like this. Even for vampires with our enhanced hearing, it was hard to hear what *anyone* had to say over the auto-tuned racket that the human youth called music.

But Juliet wasn't taking no for an answer. With a mischievous glint in her eye, she leaned in close, her lips grazing my ear as she whispered, "Come on, Mercy. You're missing all the fun. Let's show these mortals how it's really done."

A shiver ran down my spine at her proximity, her breath warm against my cool skin. I shot her a warning look, but she only grinned in response, her gaze daring me to join in. With a playful smirk, she twirled away from me, swaying sensually to the pulsing beat of the music.

Reluctantly, I followed her lead, letting the rhythm of the music guide my movements. Juliet moved with effortless grace and seduction, drawing me into her orbit with each tantalizing step. As much as I tried to resist, I found myself mirroring her dance, our bodies moving in sync as if we were one entity.

Nothing about it was choreographed. You couldn't rehearse moves like this. If my father rose from the grave and saw me now, he'd have a heart attack and die all over again. Maybe this stuff wasn't so bad after all.

Mel, sensing victory in getting me to join in, cheered and clapped, her laughter ringing out over the music. She spun around, finding the closest, hottest guy she could find. Seconds later, she was grinding him so hard I was worried she might reduce the poor mortal to dust.

As the song shifted into a slower, more sultry rhythm, Juliet's movements became more intimate, her gaze locking with mine in a silent challenge.

Caught up in the pulsating energy of the club and the hypnotic allure of Juliet's seductive dance, a rush of desire surged through me. Her every move was like a siren's call, drawing me deeper into a realm of ecstasy and temptation. The world around us faded away, leaving only the pounding music and a heat between us that two cold vampires shouldn't be able to make.

Juliet's hands traced a path along my arms, awaking my innate magic, sending sparks of electricity skittering across my skin. I could feel her breath on my neck. As the music swirled around us, I let go of all inhibitions and allowed myself to be consumed by the intoxicating spell Juliet was weaving. Each movement was a symphony of passion and yearning, drawing us closer together in a tangled web of desire.

I was losing control. Not a sensation I entertained often—because when I lost control, people turned up dead. The urge I had wasn't a desire to feed, to drain the blood from the walking meals gyrating around us. It was her... Juliet... everything about her. Her scent. Her voice. Her touch.

Our lips met in a heated kiss, the rest of the world fading away until it was only the two of us. Juliet's hands tangled in my hair, pulling me against her as our bodies moved together. I was drowning in the taste of her, the feel of her, my hunger rising in a way it never had with anyone else.

A low growl rumbled in my throat and I deepened the kiss, claiming Juliet's mouth fiercely. She returned my passion measure for measure, nails raking down my back. We were lost, ready to let the rising tide carry us away.

"Ahem."

Muggs' voice cut through the haze of desire. I pulled back from Juliet, panting, trying to clear the fog from my mind. His blind eyes were aimed at us, only a few feet away. Seeing without seeing.

"Muggs?" I asked, catching my breath. "What the hell? How'd you even make it through the crowd?"

"Everyone's dancing. Their hearts beating fast. I hear everything, Mercy. You know this. And in spirit-gaze, I can see your magic. Your aura was flashing like it was the Fourth of July."

"And you had to come for a closer look?" I shook my head. "Don't be such a perv, Muggs."

"I can't see *that*," Muggs said. "Your heart rates told me the story. You were both at a rapid five beats per minute. I wouldn't have interrupted you if it wasn't important."

I stared at Muggs for a few seconds, trying to decide if I should rip his head off for the interruption or be the understanding sire that mine used to be. "Fine. What is it, Muggs?"

"There's a disturbance in the air. Can't you feel it?"

I blinked, my senses expanding back outward. The thrum of the club's music hammered against my eardrums. The smells of alcohol and sweat washed over me.

I shrugged. "Not really."

Muggs shook his head back and forth with such force I thought it might twist right off. "My druidic senses are more in tune with nature. It's like everything all around, every tree, every blade of grass, is screaming. Something's happening. We need to check it out."

Juliet and I exchanged wearied glances and shrugged simultaneously. So much for a fun night out.

Told you so, I thought to myself, but didn't dare say it out-loud. Because, for once in my existence, I wasn't in the mood to be a bitch. *We'll check out whatever has Muggs'*

Fruit of the Looms in a wad... it's probably nothing... we'll get back to our fun.

Juliet and I followed Muggs outside, leaving Mel on the dance floor with yet *another* guy who was clearly obsessed with her... courtesy of her general cuteness, enhanced by her vampiric allure.

As we stepped out of the club, the pulsing beat of the music faded and was replaced by the distant sounds of police sirens and howling dogs.

A red glow hung over the alley. A glance upward told me why.

The moon was red as blood, swollen like an over-watered tomato.

Muggs tilted his head up, as if he could see the ominous moon. "Feel that? There's an energy flowing from the moon. It's upsetting the spirits of the place."

"It's just a moon, Muggs. Not the first blood moon that's risen in the sky in my century-plus and won't be the last. Nothing supernatural about it."

It was the truth. Blood moons usually invoke a lot of weird *human* behaviors. Apocalyptic preachers, conspiracy theorists, shit like that. Nothing that ever gave me cause to worry. Still, Muggs was usually right about this kind of thing.

"There are blood moons, Mercy, and then there are *blood* moons."

I met Juliet's gaze. She raised one skeptical eyebrow.

"Come on, Muggs. What's the worst that can happen? Oddities in nature can upset the spirits, they mess with nature a little. Things usually go back to normal once the phenomena pass."

Muggs frowned, brow furrowing. "Don't underestimate the power of blood moons. The legends exist for a reason."

I sighed, exasperated. "Legends?"

Muggs looked at us with a seriousness that made even the surrounding shadows seem to hush in reverence. "Legends, Mercy. Legends that speak of blood moons far more sinister than the usual celestial event. Legends that tell of a time in Wales, ages ago, when a blood moon rose and revived the spirits of ancient beings intent on causing chaos and destruction in the villages nearby."

I raised an eyebrow, intrigued despite myself. "Ancient beings? What kind?"

Muggs' eyes held a flicker of concern mixed with ancient wisdom. "They were spirits of heroes and villains past. Corrupt entities that fed off fear and despair."

I snorted. "Ghost stories? Really, Muggs? I'm not saying ghosts aren't real. I've seen my share of them, and a lot worse, but most of those *legends* are cooked up horseshit, and you know it."

Muggs sighed, a deep, resonant sound that seemed to carry the weight of centuries. "Mercy, I know you're skeptical, but listen to me. This blood moon is different. The spirits of this place are not at peace tonight."

I stared up at the blood moon, its crimson light staining the night sky. The cold radiating from it sank deep into my bones.

This was no ordinary moon. Muggs was right—something sinister stirred in its glow. But that meant little. Dark energies come and go more than most people know.

"Nothing we can do about it now," I said. "It might turn up to be nothing. Something fleeting, most likely."

"No reason to let it spoil the night," Juliet added. "But we'll be ready if something goes down."

I nodded. "Thanks for the heads up, Muggs. It's probably nothing, you know. No reason to panic until there's a reason to panic."

Muggs rubbed his brow. "You're probably right. Maybe I'm overreacting."

I took the old man's hand in mine. "You're not having much fun tonight, are you?"

Muggs chuckled. "I don't know what I was thinking. I'm not big on crowds. Too many sounds, too much chaos. For someone who depends on his hearing to get around, it's jarring."

"No one's forcing you to stay here," Juliet pointed out. "You can teleport back to the Underground at any time. We took the SUV here. We can drive back when we're done."

"That's alright. I think I'll stick around a little longer." Muggs' blank eyes darted skyward. "Just in case."

Chapter 2

THE BEAT PULSED THROUGH my veins as Juliet and I spun across the dance floor, losing ourselves in the rhythm. Nearby, Mel worked her usual magic, leaving a trail of dazed men in her wake. I'd always used my natural vampiric allure to attract *meals.* Mel was using her predatory *skills* to screw with men.

Cocky, manipulative pricks. Most of them, anyway. You could just tell by the way they carried themselves. Not confident—that's attractive—but arrogant. They were the sort who catch the eye, but you know better than to expect a call from them in the morning.

Not like any men I ever took home over the years dared to call *me* the next day. For obvious reasons. But you know the type I'm talking about.

Mel was giving them a little taste of their own medicine. In *our* world—which was wherever the hell we went—we were in charge.

These men were like marionettes. Mel was the puppeteer. She was pulling every string. They couldn't resist. They'd have made her a nice all-you-can-eat man buffet. If that's what she was after.

Not a bad way to end a night, if you ask me. But we weren't there for food. The purpose was to go out and have fun. Who *doesn't* get a bite when going out at night? Who says you can't have fun *and* a meal?

I always enjoyed playing with my food.

I might have forced the issue. I could have convinced Juliet easily enough. Mel was my progeny. She'd follow my lead. We could be discreet about it.

Yet worry persisted in my mind. Muggs was still outside, anxious about strange energies and blood moons. I tried to push his warnings aside.

It was probably nothing.

Yet, it *was* the story of my existence. Without fail, *any time* I enjoyed myself or got the slightest bit relaxed, another supernatural shit show made its debut.

I was the shit show queen. I don't know who died, or got staked, and designated me the heiress to oppose all things evil. I mean, I was evil myself. A little bit evil, anyway. I was hardly the little church girl daddy raised me to be.

If the world had any idea how many times I'd saved their asses, they'd throw me a parade. Maybe send me flowers. Blood lilies, ideally. That still wouldn't be enough. Not like I was asking for a show of appreciation.

I just wanted a fucking day off. And by "day" I mean a lifetime. A good century to cool off, to do whatever the hell I wanted, with no monstrous interference.

Is that too much to ask for? No world-devouring monsters, please. No assholes dead set on world denomination. My god, I'm *sick* of that crap. Don't the bad guys realize that's a lot of responsibility to take on? Ruling the world sounds like a big, steamy pile of stress.

If any deities out there are listening, I'm officially putting in my request. I should have a few centuries of vacation time built up. Find someone to fill my shoes for a while. I'm going to the beach. Not to sun bathe, of course. I don't have a death wish. But nights with my toes in the sand, moonlight cast over the ocean, and a clean breeze...

And a Bloody Mary. O-negative on the rocks.

Yes, please.

Juliet was right. I *deserved* a night—or a thousand nights—to do nothing but enjoy myself. To enjoy time with my people.

I tried to push the worry from my mind as the song shifted into a heavier beat and the crowd surged with excitement. Juliet flashed me a wicked grin, red eyes reflecting the strobes.

I spun Juliet out, pulling her back against me as we moved to the music. Mel had some poor fool practically drooling all over himself as she whispered in his ear.

Then a scream pierced the pounding beat. Wide-eyed with terror, a woman stumbled back from the crowd, pointing at something I couldn't see.

More screams followed. The crowd parted, scrambling away from... *something.*

I cursed under my breath, grabbing Juliet's hand to pull her with me as I pushed through the panicked crowd.

My barely beating heart dropped when I saw what had them so terrified.

Ghosts.

A whole horde of them. Pale, flickering figures drifting through the walls and descending on the crowd.

"Well, son of a bitch!" Just what I needed. I fumbled for the wand strapped to my thigh, snatching it free to wave it at the ghosts.

"*Recedo!*"

It was a spell I rarely used. It couldn't *kill* ghosts. You can't kill what's already dead? It didn't banish them either. I wasn't totally sure it would work on *these* ghosts. Not every spirit is the same. But the spell had a generic quality, usually good to repel energy-based entities. Temporarily, anyway.

People stampeded for the exits, trampling each other while fleeing the spirits. I glimpsed Mel trying to herd people toward the door, to help them escape, but in the chaos I lost sight of her.

I fought back a shiver of unease as the ghosts drew closer, their formless eyes fixed on me with eerie intent. The air crackled with suppressed energy as I focused my magic, repelling as many ghosts as I could. Trying to steer them away from the humans.

But they weren't interested in the humans. They were focused on *us*. They were coming at Juliet and me. Targeting *us*.

What had I ever done to piss off dead people?

But maybe it wasn't about me. It was about *our kind*. Did they see us as kin, dead but not quite? Were they pissed off we'd cheated the system? That we escaped the whatever-there-was that awaited souls after death, whatever they'd suffered since their lived ended?

"*Recedo! Recedo! Recedo!*"

The spirits coming at Juliet and me bounced off the azure magic that spun out of my wand. I diverted them away from us—and toward the doors. Where I'd last seen Mel.

Shit.

"Mel, get out of there!" I wasn't sure she heard me. The cacophony of screams and the thunderous beat of the club's music swallowed my voice. I finally caught sight of her—just in time to see her eyes flash with the sickly green hue of the ghosts themselves.

"No!" Panic clawed at my chest. "Mel! Fight it!"

But I couldn't go to her. More ghosts swarmed toward me, their hollow eyes fixed on mine. I raised my wand again, channeling all the magic I could muster. "Recedo! Recedo!"

"Mercy! I think they're here for us!" Juliet was clutching my arm so hard that she might leave bruises if I were a mere mortal.

"Stay close," I said, gritting my teeth as I blasted another ghost away. "I can repel them... probably."

"Probably? What about Mel? And where the hell is Muggs?"

I glanced back to where I'd last seen Mel. Screaming and crimson showers in the air. She'd lost control. A human ghost in a vampire's body? They'd never be able to handle our... *cravings.* Combine *that* with whatever angst they brought with them from the afterlife and it was a recipe for carnage.

Not a recipe you'd likely find in your grandma's cookbook.

Suddenly, a flash of green light heralded Muggs' arrival. He teleported in, eyes scanning the chaos with a horrified expression.

"Muggs!" I shouted over the din. "Mel's possessed, and I can't hold them off much longer! Can you teleport us the hell out of here?"

Before he could respond, a ghost lunged at him, phasing right through his body. His eyes flared with that same sinister brightness as Mel's.

"Not you too, Muggs..." Desperation gripped me, but I couldn't afford to panic. Ghosts were closing in from all sides, their ethereal forms reaching for me.

"Recedo!" I cast again and again, each spell sapping more of my strength. My vision blurred; sweat trickled down my forehead.

"Mercy, behind you!" Juliet's scream snapped me back.

Twirling just in time, I fended off another spirit and stumbled backward into Juliet. "We need to get out of here!"

"Recedo!" I cast again, pushing back another cluster of ghosts hovering near the DJ booth. I scanned the room. For a moment, it seemed like the spirits had retreated, fleeing through walls and disappearing into the night.

"Juliet, we need to—" I turned to her, grabbing her arm. "They got to Mel and Muggs! We have to get them before they kill too many—"

The sight of her face sucked the breath right out of my chest. Her eyes, usually like two rubies, now held a subtle, eerie, and sickly light.

"No... they got you too..." My voice was barely audible over the surrounding chaos.

The voice that emerged from Juliet's lips wasn't hers. It was deeper, colder, filled with ancient malice. "We're taking all of your kind. In service of our Emperor."

"Emperor?" I repeated, shock freezing me in place for a fraction of a second. Then survival instincts kicked in. I twirled around, wand at the ready, just in time to fend off another ghost darting my direction.

"Get away from me, fucker!" I shouted, casting another spell. When I spun back around, Juliet was gone. The sound of screams through the crowd told me what I needed to know. She'd joined Mel in her... eviscerations.

"Shit," I cursed under my breath. I had to keep fighting off these damn ghosts while watching my friends—now enemies—tear through innocent people.

"Think, Mercy, think!" I muttered, trying to come up with a plan. I couldn't let this continue, but every time I tried to move closer to them, another ghost got in my way. Could I exorcise these ghosts? What if I blasted my spell down their throats? What would that do?

"Dammit!" I cursed, frustration boiling over. Out of the corner of my eye, I saw Mel's possessed form toss aside another lifeless body. My heart clenched, but I couldn't afford to lose focus. If I did, I'd be next.

"Help! Somebody!" A frantic voice called out. It was one of the club-goers, huddled behind an overturned table. I wanted to help them, but every time I took another step, another ghost got in the way.

"Stay down!" I yelled back, hoping they'd listen. I had to find a way out before it was too late. But as I looked around, all I saw was chaos. People screaming, bodies hitting the floor, and in the center of it all, my friends—no, my family—enthralled by the dead.

All to serve an... emperor? Was *that* what the ghost inside Juliet actually said? I could think about *that* later. I couldn't last much longer. More ghosts appeared by the second. They weren't interested in the *humans*.

They'd come for us. But why?

"Think, Mercy," I urged myself again. I couldn't fight them all. Not like this. I needed to regroup, to come up with a plan. But first, I had to get out of here alive. Well, as alive as I could be. Without some dead bastard's spirit clawing its way into my psyche.

"Recedo!" I cast one last spell, forcing a path through the sea of ghosts. I bolted for the exit, shoving past panicked humans and ducking under flailing limbs. There was nothing else I could do. Mel, Muggs, and Juliet had reduced the night club to an all-you-can-eat vampire buffet.

If I tried to stop them, I'd open myself up to being possessed, too. If that happened, there'd be no one left to *save* my friends.

"Shit," I looked into the night sky as I burst out of the club. Spirits swirled in the sky, their ghastly forms illuminated by the blood moon. Hundreds of them. Thousands, maybe. They noticed me immediately, their hollow eyes locking onto me like predators spotting prey.

No sense casting more spells. I couldn't repel *all of them*.

So I ran. As fast as I could—which, as a vampire, was pretty damn speedy. I reached the SUV and, fumbling with the keys, I unlocked the door.

I drove through the deserted streets, my mind racing. I had to get to the Underground. I needed help, and fast.

Chapter 3

As I hopped out of the SUV, the chill of the underground parking garage seeped through my leather boots. The eerie quiet felt wrong. It was the middle of the night. I almost always ran into someone coming or going from the secure entrance and exit. As quiet as it was, you'd think it was noon. When you wouldn't catch a vampire dead, undead, and certainly not *alive* coming or going.

"Something's off," I muttered, jogging to the elevator. The hand-print scanner glowed blue, recognizing me instantly. The metal doors slid open with a hiss, and the familiar scent of aged stone and incense wafted out. I stepped inside, tapping my foot impatiently as the elevator descended.

"Come on, come on." The weight of worry about Mel, Muggs, and Juliet pressed down on my shoulders. If these ghosts were seeking *vampires,* how could we stop them? I was the only witch in the group. I couldn't do it alone.

The doors opened to an empty corridor. More quiet. I glanced around. Nothing. No one. The silence was deafening. I sprinted down the hallway, my footsteps echoing ominously against the stone walls.

"Hello? Antoine? Clement?" My voice bounced back at me, mocking my growing panic.

I checked the throne room. Empty. The common area and training rooms. Deserted. Even the usually bustling orphanage was still.

"Alright, think, Mercy. Where would they go?" I needed answers, and I needed them fast. My feet carried me to the security room, where Mel practically lived. If there were any clues, they'd be there.

The door creaked open, revealing a chaotic mess of monitors and security feeds. Mel's tablet lay discarded on the desk, its screen cracked but functional. I snatched it up, fingers flying across the interface to pull up the feeds.

"What happened? Where did everyone go?"

There they were, captured in pixelated clarity. Antoine, Clement, Ian and the vampire orphans—all of them. Their eyes glowed, their movements jerky and uncoordinated.

"Possessed," I spat, a sick realization settling in my gut. Ghosts had taken over their bodies, and now they were marching out of the Underground like some twisted parade.

"Fuck!" The word exploded out of me as I slammed the tablet onto the desk, sending it skidding across the glossy surface. My pulse hammered in my ears, and a red haze clouded my vision.

"Goddammit, Mercy, pull it together," I muttered to myself, but the boiling rage wasn't having any of it. Before I knew it, I was storming down the labyrinthine hallways of the Underground towards the throne room, each step echoing with the fury of a tyrannosaurus rex.

When I burst into the throne room, the ostentatious opulence of the place made my blood boil even hotter. Velvet couches, gilded mirrors, chandeliers dripping with crystals—what a goddamn joke. Living in the *sewers* and acting like royalty. Who the hell did we think we were?

"Useless, all of it!" I snarled, zeroing in on one of the velvet couches. With a guttural scream, I lifted the heavy piece of furniture and hurled it against the wall. It shattered into splinters and fabric, scattering like shrapnel around the room.

"Potential stakes," I whispered, eyes locking onto the jagged wooden remains. An idea sparked, wild and desperate. "Staking them might work... but would it expel the spirits? Or just send their souls to vampire hell?"

"How the hell does ghost possession even work?" I wondered aloud, pacing through the debris. My mind spun with questions and half-formed theories. Was there a way to separate the ghosts from their hosts without killing my friends?

I'd seen a thousand or more ghosts swirling in the deathly light of the blood moon. Were they *all* seeking vampires to possess? I couldn't exactly stake every vampire in existence. Not while trying to avoid getting possessed, myself. It wasn't practical and it might not save them. A stake sent *vampire* spirits to hell. It might do nothing but leave the ghosts in full control of their stolen bodies. Or it could save them.

I could try it. An experiment, maybe. But even if it worked, I'd need help.

Then it hit me, like a punch to the gut. Annabelle Mulledy. The acting voodoo queen in New Orleans. She was the one person I knew who had ever shared her body with a ghost.

"Of course," I said, rolling my eyes at the universe's sick sense of humor. Annabelle and I rarely saw eye to eye. Our history was a tangled mess of grudging respect and mutual disdain. But if anyone knew how to deal with this kind of supernatural clusterfuck, it was her.

"Great," I sighed, pinching the bridge of my nose. "Just fucking great." The last thing I wanted was to ask Annabelle for help, but what choice did I have? My family was out there, possessed by vengeful spirits. Spouting crap about some emperor ghost or whatever. I didn't know what *that* was about when the ghost inside Juliet said it—but I knew it meant the ghosts had come for a purpose. They had an agenda.

Annabelle's story had always been one hell of a cautionary tale. It all started back on her family's plantation during the antebellum period. Some disastrously executed voodoo spell gone awry. A cursed bloodline, a revival of a dead caplata girl, and an attack on Annabelle's family. She ended up possessed by the spirit of Isabelle, a slave girl who'd died on the plantation. The sister of the voodoo caplata who'd tried to bring her younger sister back from the dead—in Annabelle's body.

Of course, Annabelle being Annabelle, she managed to turn a shitshow into a superpower. Initially, they were at each other's throats—more than literally speaking, since they shared the same body. But eventually, they figured out how to coexist. They even learned how to untangle their spirits. But they realized that together, they were stronger than apart.

When they were bound, Annabelle and Isabelle had access to some serious mojo—namely, Beli, the gatekeeper dragon-spirit. This wasn't just any dragon either. Beli manifested as a spirit dagger, glowing with green energy. When she summoned him on earth, anyway. Supposedly in the dragon's native realm he'd appear in his natural form whenever she called his name.

The dagger also had trans-dimensional properties. Annabelle could wield it to slice through the fabric of space and time. Other dimensions? No problem. Time travel? Not exactly a piece of cake, but possible.

Beli was also terrifying. If a vampire got cut by the dragon-blade, it sent us straight to vampire hell. Direct to vampire hell. Couldn't even collect a hundred dollars by passing go. And when *that* happened, it didn't leave any bodies behind. There was no "un-staking" a victim of Annabelle's blade. It was a one-way-ticket to the dark place.

"Annabelle fucking Mulledy." I shook my head as I pulled out my phone. "You'd better pick up."

I punched Annabelle's number into my phone with more force than necessary. It was a wonder I didn't crack my damn screen. Each digit felt like a betrayal of my pride, but desperate times called for desperate measures. The phone rang once, twice, and then clicked.

"Mercy Brown. To what do I owe the displeasure?" Annabelle's voice oozed with that Southern charm she wielded like a weapon. Underneath it, though, was steel. She didn't like me any more than I liked her, but there was mutual respect buried under layers of animosity.

"Annabelle, let's skip the pleasantries," I snapped, pacing back and forth in the empty security room. My eyes flicked to the shattered couch, its splintered remains a testament to my earlier outburst. "We've got a problem. A big one."

"Of course you do," she replied dryly. "Why else would you be calling?"

"Ghosts are possessing vampires. It has something to do with the blood moon. I might be the only one left. I need your help."

"What was that you just said?" Annabelle chuckled through the phone. "I could *swear* I just heard you ask for *help*."

"Cut the crap, Annabelle." I stopped pacing. "You know I don't enjoy doing this. I wouldn't ask if I had anywhere else to turn."

"True," she conceded, her tone losing some of its edge. "But why should I help you? I haven't heard from you in months, and it's not like I don't have enough on my plate as it is."

"Because you're not an idiot," I shot back. "You know that if these spirits gain control over a bunch of vampires, it's game over. Not just for me, but for all of us. And last I checked, you live in the vampire capital of North America. If this shit hasn't hit you yet, you'd better believe it's coming. And it'll be a hundred times worse in New Orleans than it is in Providence when it does."

"Fair point," she said after a pause. "Alright, Mercy. I'll help. But on one condition."

"Name it," I growled, already dreading whatever insane demand she'd come up with.

"I'm bringing Pauli with me."

"I expected as much," I added. "Sure, you can cut portals through time and dimensions, but you can't teleport within the same dimension. He was just up here with Hailey a few weeks back. I can deal with Pauli."

"Hold tight, Mercy. Isabelle, Pauli and I will be there soon. And remember, you asked for this. And you owe me one." The line went dead before I could offer a snappy retort.

"Great. Just great," I muttered, shoving the phone back into my pocket. I took a deep breath, trying to calm the storm brewing inside me. I *owe* her one? This was about saving people's lives. She was a freaking saint in the eyes of most compared to *me*. Why not do this out of the goodness of her heart? Why should I owe Annabelle Mulledy shit?

Whatever. Help was on the way. If I had to swallow my pride and put up with Annabelle's crap to save my friends, so be it.

Chapter 4

I headed to the throne room to await Annabelle's arrival. I'd almost forgotten that I'd trashed the place. Its once pristine walls were now marred by the remnants of my earlier outburst. I stood amidst the wreckage, nursing the throbbing in my temples. I was about to send Annabelle a text asking her what was taking so long when the air shimmered with an explosion of rainbow light.

Pauli's signature entrance. He was draped over Annabelle's neck like a feather boa—but without the feathers. He was the real thing. Just as glamorous (in his own mind) and twice as creepy.

"What the hell happened here?" Annabelle furrowed her brow as she took in the splintered wood and scattered cushions. "Was there a fight?"

"Yeah," I snorted. "The sofa got lippy. I kicked its ass."

"Dayum bitch!" Pauli snickered, his scales glinting in the dim light. "The couch spends its entire existence getting nothing but ass. One ass after the next. It gives you a little *lip* and you tear it apart?"

"Damn straight." I huffed.

"You show that lippy couch who's boss! Make an example out of it so the other couches know and learn to take that ass like a champ!"

"Did that." I crossed my arms over my chest. "Now, are we going to figure out how to save my friends and end this shit or what?"

Annabelle's expression softened slightly, but her eyes remained sharp. "Ghost possession is a tricky thing. Most of the time, if a ghost possesses a human, the host has to consent to allow the invading spirit to take the reins."

"Yeah, well, it's not the same in this situation," I said, pacing the room. "Mel, Juliet, Muggs—they wouldn't consent. The ghosts forced their way into them. Took over straight away."

"That's troubling." Annabelle's face darkened. "It could be because vampires don't have souls. Baron Samedi holds your souls from the moment you're turned. For most of your kind, at least, that's how it works. Without a soul, the vampire's spirit that owns the body is at a disadvantage to the invading ghosts. That *might* be why these ghosts are seeking vampires to possess rather than humans."

"Fang-fucking-tastic," I muttered under my breath. Pauli hissed sympathetically from his perch on Annabelle's neck.

"There's also a chance," Annabelle continued, her tone skeptical, "that once the blood moon ends—since it's a lunar eclipse, it shouldn't last long—that this will pass."

"You really think that's likely?" I asked. "Because in my experience, when something nasty goes to lengths like this, it isn't so they can take a joy ride for a couple hours, then go back to where they came from."

"I don't think it's likely," she said bluntly. "It's more likely that the blood moon triggered some kind of ancient magic that revived the spirits. And now that they're here, blood moon or not, they're here to stay."

"We have to assume the worst then—that this isn't just going to pass."

"Agreed," Annabelle replied.

"Juliet's ghost mentioned something about an emperor," I said, my mind racing. "The ghost said they were targeting vampires, so they *knew* what they were doing before they came back. It's not much, but it's something."

"Emperor?" Annabelle shook her head, her expression thoughtful but dubious. "Do you know how many empires have risen and fallen over the millennia?"

"True, but if these spirits are all connected to this emperor somehow, and they had an agenda to go after vampires, it must mean they didn't resurrect at random." I paused, considering. "Someone orchestrated this with the intention of bringing back a particular emperor's spirit and other ghosts loyal to him."

"Sounds like a dick," Pauli interjected, his forked tongue flickering out as he spoke. "Can we narrow down which emperor we're talkin' about? Maybe it's Caligula! I hear he was *all* kinds of fun!"

I cocked an eyebrow. "The one who married his sister? The same Caligula who commissioned virgins to swim naked in his pool and nibble at his junk as he swam by?"

"Male virgins!" Pauli nodded. "Like I said. All *kinds* of fun!"

I took a deep breath. It took every ounce of restraint I had to resist the urge to punch Pauli in the face. He could be entertaining in small doses—when you hadn't just had everyone you care about get *possessed* by ancient ghosts.

"It could be anyone, not necessarily a Roman emperor," Annabelle said, snapping her fingers as if she'd had a sudden revelation. "But we *can* find out. We need to capture at least one of your friends and bring them back. Get them to talk."

"Capture and interrogate my friends?" I snapped. "These ghosts will not tell us what we want to know without a little torture. My friends are still in there, somewhere."

"You're right," Annabelle said with a nod. "Whenever I gave Isabelle the reins, I could see, hear, and *feel* everything she did. I'm not going to sugarcoat it. This won't be easy for them. But what if the roles were reversed? Would you rather let some invasive spirit take over your existence, or want your friends to do whatever it takes to free you? Even if it meant... pain?"

I sighed. "Fine. But torture is a last option."

"Don't see the problem," Pauli added. "You *are* vampires. You can heal from damn near anything."

"Pain is still pain!" I shouted. "There's a reason they call it *torture*. I can't do that to Juliet, or Mel... not even Muggs or Antoine."

"Leave the torture to me," Pauli said. "I know how to make torture *fun* for the whole family!"

I grunted. I didn't know how to respond to something like that? I knew that leather, chains, and nipple clamps were a part of Pauli's regular Friday-night repertoire, but the whole *'fun for the whole family'* comment... what the fuck?

"Whatever," I relented. "But if we're going to do this, we need to get to it fast. Because even if we capture one of them, and even if we learn the emperor's identity, that doesn't mean history has any record of the dark magic said emperor might have used relative to a blood moon and his return in the 21st century."

"Fair point," Annabelle said, her eyes narrowing as she considered the stakes. "But unless you have a better idea, we're running out of time."

"Do you?" I shot back. "Have a better idea?"

Annabelle took a deep breath and exhaled slowly. "I could start stabbing people with Beli and see what happens."

"Absolutely not!" I screamed. "We don't know what would happen. You'd send my friends to vampire hell with no way back!"

"Plan A, then?" Annabelle tilted her head, an amused glint in her eyes.

"It could be a colossal waste of time," I said. "But you're right. Any other options we have at our disposal involve... *experimentation.* I like that even less."

Annabelle popped her knuckles. "And lest you forget, Mercy, we have until sunrise before this gets a lot more difficult. They'll have to take cover during the day and your movements will be likewise limited."

I rolled my eyes. "I've been a vampire longer than you've been alive several times over, Annabelle. I know how it works."

"Just saying," Annabelle said with a nod. "We can waste what time we have talking about it or we can go catch ourselves a possessed vampire."

Chapter 5

The blood moon hung overhead like a sinister omen as I pulled out of the Underground in one of our black SUVs, Annabelle riding shotgun and Pauli—now shifted into human form—in the back. A crimson light cast swallowed up the city like a whale might engulf a disobedient prophet. It hadn't changed a bit since the last I saw it. Certainly not normal. Usually an eclipse lasted a few hours—and a total lunar eclipse only thirty minutes, an hour at most.

I clenched my hands on the steering wheel. "Why the hell is this blood moon overstaying its welcome?"

Annabelle was scrolling through her phone. "It's certainly unusual, Mercy. The longest blood moon on record happened just a few years back in 2018. It lasted an hour and forty minutes. I'm guessing based on the time you called me earlier, and what time it is currently, we've exceeded that by now—"

I glanced at the clock on the dashboard. "I don't remember what time it was when we were at the club. But you're right. It's been almost two hours, maybe longer. What could that mean?"

"Something bad," Pauli interrupted, scratching his head. "Naughty, naughty, moon. Reminds me of this pasty white boy I used to date. After a night with me, it took hours before the red was gone."

Annabelle let out a chuckle at Pauli's comment, but her eyes remained serious as she peered out the window at the blood moon. "We can only speculate on what this extended eclipse might signify, but one thing is certain – it's not natural. And from what I could tell online, there isn't *supposed* to be a lunar eclipse right now."

I gripped the wheel tighter, my knuckles almost glowing in the dim light of the SUV. Annabelle was right – this wasn't just your run-of-the-mill celestial event. The blood moon lingered in the sky like a festering wound. If it wasn't because of an eclipse something *supernatural* was at work. It wasn't just some kind of an ancient spell that *used* the energy of a blood moon, but somehow, someone *caused* the moon itself to radiate a hue I'd otherwise find appetizing.

"There's only one explanation," Pauli said with more monotone in his voice than I was used to. "We're talking about the fifth dimension. The middle ground between light and shadow. The place that lies between the pit of man's fears and the summit of his knowledge. The dimension of imagination. It is an area which we call the—"

"It's not the goddamn Twilight Zone!" I interrupted.

"Doo doo doo doo doo doo doo doo!"

"SHUT UP, PAULI," Annabelle and I shouted in unison. I smiled a little. Pauli was probably Annabelle's best friend. But even *she* could only take so much of his untimely bullshit. For once, Annabelle and I were on the same page.

"Seriously, I need to concentrate!" I insisted, my voice firm. "I can't find Juliet right now. I don't know where all the possessed vampires from the Underground might be. I *made* Mel and Muggs. I can use our sire-progeny bond to find them, but it takes total focus."

With Pauli momentarily silenced, I gripped the steering wheel tighter. The SUV roared through the empty streets, each jolt and bump making me more aware of the stakes we were up against. The city was eerily quiet under the blood moon's ominous glow, as if it sensed the dangers lurking in its shadows.

My connection with Mel and Muggs tugged at my consciousness like a taut wire, pulling me toward them. It was a subtle but compelling sensation. It wasn't easy to follow while driving. The streets didn't always lead straight where I wanted. When my sire-bond moved from my brow to my temple, I knew I had to turn. Seeing a street heading in the direction I needed, I wrenched the wheel. The tires screeched in protest, but the SUV complied, barreling down an alleyway that looked like it hadn't seen sunlight in decades.

"Jesus, Mercy." Annabelle clenched onto the handle on the passenger door. "We aren't all immortal vampires. We can't just walk away from a car accident without a scratch."

"Sorry." I wasn't really sorry, but it was easier to apologize than respond. I couldn't afford the distraction. We were getting close.

The pull had gravitated back to my brow once we hit the narrow alley. Then it abruptly shifted again as we passed an unremarkable metal door in the side of a brick building.

"They're in there."

"You sure?" Annabelle asked.

I nodded. "But they aren't alone."

"You can sense *other* vampires?" Pauli asked.

I shook my head. "I can smell the blood. Even from inside the car. It's that strong."

Annabelle cocked an eyebrow. "The blood?"

I nodded. "They're feasting."

"Gross," Pauli muttered, wrinkling his nose. "Let's get this over with."

We piled out of the SUV. I turned to each of them. "Remember, we aren't here to fight. We grab Muggs or

Mel. Both of them, if possible. And we get the hell out of here."

Pauli nodded. "Easy enough. If I can see them, I can zap over to them, give them a little squeeze, and take them straight back to the base. Unless they're standing next to each other, though, I'll have to make two trips to get both."

"Or three," I added. "If you see Juliet in there, take her. If we don't get Mel or Muggs this time, I can track them later. It won't be as easy to track down Juliet later."

Annabelle tilted her head. "Are you sure we should grab all of them?"

I stared at her blankly. "If we can get them back, why the hell not?"

"Because these ghosts are up to something. You mentioned an emperor before. Emperors are all about building empires. If they're traveling together, it makes sense to leave at least one of your progenies inside. It'll make it a hell of a lot easier to track them down later."

My jaw tightened at Annabelle's words. She had a point, as much as I hated to admit it. The possibility of leaving behind one of my progenies was a bitter pill to swallow. But in the world we navigated, sacrifices were often necessary to ensure the survival of the rest.

"Fine," I relented, my voice clipped with tension. "Grab whoever you can first, Pauli. Come back for Juliet, if she's there and you have an opportunity. But we'll leave either

Mel or Muggs behind for now. Until we know more about what we're facing."

With a plan in place—I pressed open the door. The smell of blood, already strong from the alley, hit me like a wall as soon as we stepped inside. My fangs throbbed in response. It was like walking into a steakhouse.

"So many victims..." I sighed.

"We should try and save those we can," Annabelle whispered back. "While Pauli is doing his thing. A little rescue might provide the distraction he needs."

My hand clenched around my wand. "I don't know. We can try. But there are too many people here to count."

"Every life counts."

I nodded back at Annabelle. Leave it to a human to prioritize saving lives. I tried to minimize bloodshed too but as a vampire... well... saving humans was secondary. Sort of like how saving your dog from a house fire comes *after* getting the family to safety.

Not that humans were dogs. More like cattle. But still valuable. And as a former-human, myself, the better part of me understood Annabelle's concern. Humans still held a special place in my undead heart. Nostalgia is funny that way.

"You're right," I whispered. "But if these ghosts are still seeking and possessing more vampires, and this emperor has empire-level aspirations, this is just the beginning. The primary objective is recovering Mel or Muggs, or *someone* who can tell us more about what we're dealing with. If we save a few humans in the process, so be it."

"I'm shifting now," Pauli announced. "Grab my clothes, Annabelle. Or don't. I'm fine coming back without them."

I glanced at Annabelle. "Grab his clothes. No one wants to see that."

With a pulse of multi-colored light, Pauli returned to his boa constrictor form and slithered out from what used to be the neck of his shirt. Annabelle had a backpack and quickly tossed his clothes inside. She'd come prepared. After working with Pauli a few times myself, I'd also learned the same lesson. If you don't want a naked Pauli following you around—and who wants that?—you'd best make sure he has a change of clothes at the ready at all times.

We navigated through a labyrinth of boxes and broken machinery, drawn deeper into the belly of the beast. The fragrance of blood grew stronger, mingling with the stale air and dust.

As we rounded a corner, the full horror of the scene unfolded before us. Hundreds of vampires and just as many humans were tangled together in a grotesque tableau. Blood splattered everywhere, pooling on the grimy floor and streaking the walls. The vampires' eyes glowed a sickly green, the ghosts possessing them clearly struggling to control their bloodlust.

"Sweet mother of darkness." I'd never seen *anything* this grotesque and delicious all at once. I was as horrified as I was tempted. I swallowed my carnal instincts and focused instead on the greater implication of what was unfolding. I recognized most of the vampires, some of them were older than me. But they were behaving like younglings. The ghosts driving their bodies didn't know how to manage their cravings. That spelled bad news for everyone. All the strength and speed of *experienced* vampires with none of the control. "This... This is worse than I imagined."

"Mercy," Annabelle's voice quivered. She clasped a hand over her mouth, her face paling to an alarming degree. "I think I'm gonna—"

"Don't you dare vomit," I snapped, grabbing her shoulder and shaking her gently. "We need to keep it together. Look at me."

Annabelle gulped, nodding. "Okay, okay. Focus."

"Good girl." I turned my attention back to the chaos, scanning the crowd. Many of the vampires there were part of my team. But now, they were behaving like feral younglings, gluttonous and wild.

"Pauli, see Mel or Muggs?" I whispered. "Juliet?"

"Not yet," Pauli replied through our telepathic bond, his snake form allowing him to slink unnoticed through the crowd.

I continued scanning. Motion caught my eye. The only vampire in the crowd of possessed monsters who moved with something resembling grace.

It was Mel, scantily clad, stepping through the throng with a regal air that wasn't hers. She was attended by other vampires, including Muggs, who referred to her as "Emperor."

"Well, shit," I muttered under my breath. "That's not good."

"Mercy, what do we do?" Annabelle asked, her voice barely above a whisper.

"Pauli, you see Mel? She's the leader. The Emperor. We need to get her."

"On it," Pauli responded. "Here vampy, vampy, vamp. Daddy's on the way."

In a flash of rainbow colors, Pauli disappeared, reappearing over Mel's shoulders. But before he could wrap around her, a blast of unearthly energy sent him flying off. He hit the ground hard, his luminescent serpentine form skidding across the blood-slick floor.

"Intruders!" Mel—or rather, Emperor Whoever—shouted, her voice echoing with an unnatural resonance. She began ordering the other possessed vampires to assemble, their movements jerky and disjointed but terrifyingly fast.

"Annabelle, get ready," I warned, adrenaline surging through my veins. "This is about to get ugly."

"Ugly's my middle name," Annabelle muttered, popping her knuckles.

I chuckled. "You said it. Not me."

"Not what I meant!"

I winked at Annabelle and twirled my wand between my fingers. "Remember, don't stab my friends. We're saving these vampires. Not consigning them to hell."

"Your position is noted.," Annabelle narrowed her eyes and summoned her spirit-blade. "Beli!"

The air shimmered, and a dagger wreathed in green energy materialized in her hand. She gripped it tightly, ready for the impending clash.

"Annabelle! I *just* said…"

Annabelle shrugged. "You expect me to fight unarmed? Screw that!"

Damn it. She had a point—but I still didn't want to lose anyone to that damned blade of hers. But I'd brought her here. How could I ask her *not* to defend herself? And how *else* could she fight back against a brood of bloodthirsty spirit-possessed vampires?

Muggs—or whatever was pretending to be him—lunged at us. He was blind, but the spirit within him didn't have any problem zeroing in on us. Somehow. But the ghost also didn't know what it was doing. He was attempting to wield druid magic with all the finesse of a drunk toddler.

Vines erupted from the ground, but they were weak, tangled messes. I countered them with a simple spell, my wand slicing through the air like an extension of my will.

"Nice try, asshole," I spat, deflecting his attacks with ease. "Pauli, get Annabelle out of here. Now."

"On it, boss lady," Pauli replied, slithering back into his human form, though his skin still shimmered with iridescent hues. He wrapped an arm around Annabelle. "Come on, girl. Time to skedaddle."

"Mercy, seriously?" Annabelle shouted as Pauli teleported them away in another flash of rainbow light.

I was a little surprised that Pauli followed my order. He was more loyal to Annabelle than me. But he knew what I did—as many vampires as we were about to face, she couldn't hold them off forever. Not even with the aid of her dragon dagger.

No longer distracted by the Annabelle predicament, I turned my full attention to Muggs. The ghost inside him snarled, trying to cast another spell, but I was faster.

"*Enerva*!" My spell hit its mark. Muggs' body convulsed and then went limp, collapsing to the ground.

"Gotcha," I whispered, a sense of grim satisfaction settling over me. But there was no time to celebrate. The crowd of nearly feral vampires was closing in, their eyes glowing that sickly green. Mel was shouting at them, but they were having a hard time following orders. They were more interested in their *meals* than me.

I scanned the horde for any sign of Juliet. She had to be there... somewhere...

I'd spotted Antoine in the fray. Clement and several of the orphans. Most of my team. With Juliet's bright pink hair, she usually stuck out in a crowd like a sore thumb. Where the hell was she?

Maybe her hair was blood-stained and blended in. Maybe she wasn't there. Trying to find her in the crowd was a like a three-dimensional version of *Where's Waldo*. With a lot more carnage than I'd ever noticed in any of those books.

Antoine came at me. He was moving on all fours, as if he'd forgotten he was a biped.

I cocked an eyebrow. "Really? *Enerva.*"

Antoine fell to the ground, face planting in a pool of blood.

"Sleep tight, buddy."

Finally, in another burst of prismatic colors, Pauli reappeared. "Can't get Mel. She has some kind of magic."

"Muggs is unconscious." I pointed at him with my wand. "Take him back to headquarters. I'll meet you there in twenty."

No smart ass, inappropriate response. Not a single crude joke. The scene was so damn traumatizing that even Pauli was in shock. He did as I asked, wrapping himself around Muggs' incapacitated body. Another flash of rainbow light and they were gone.

I took one last, desperate glance around, hoping against hope to find Juliet. But the chaotic sea of bloodthirsty, ghost-possessed vampires offered no solace. With a frustrated growl, I turned on my heel and sprinted back to the exit.

"Mercy!" Annabelle's voice cut through the cacophony as I reached the SUV. She was already in the passenger seat, her face pale but determined. "We need to go, now!"

"On it," I said, yanking open the driver's door and sliding in. My hands shook as I jammed the key into the ignition, but the engine roared to life on the first try. A minor miracle, considering our luck tonight.

"Did you see Juliet?" Annabelle asked, her voice tight with worry.

"Not a damned trace," I replied, slamming the gearshift into drive. The tires screeched as we peeled out, leaving the chaotic scene behind us. "But we'll find her. Pauli took Muggs back to the Underground."

Annabelle's eyes widened. "You sure he's safe? With a possessed vampire?"

I nodded. "Muggs is unconscious. He should be down for a few hours. We'll have to wait before we can interrogate him, which isn't ideal, but I didn't have any other choice. How Mel shocked Pauli, before, I wasn't sure if Muggs would do the same to him."

Annabelle was still clutching Beli in her hand and trembling. I'd never seen her so... scared. The big, bad,

Annabelle Mulledy. She'd faced off against demigods and won. But that much blood, so many bodies unlikely to recover... it had an effect.

I hit the gas and sped out of the alley and back onto the streets. "You don't need that blade any more. We're safe."

Annabelle shook her head. "I don't know. I can't stop seeing those bodies. All that blood. The vampires. They were ruthless."

"They're behaving like ferals," I said. "Younglings out of control. This is going to get worse before it gets better. But at least we'll be able to track their leader. So long as the emperor, or whatever he is, is using her, I'll know where they are."

Annabelle released her blade, but her eyes remained focused on her hand where it was moments before. "Isabelle is afraid, too. She said that these ghosts are strong. And she's the most powerful spirit I've ever met, so that means something. There's an ancient magic they've brought back with them. Something we've never seen."

I sighed. "Let's just hope whichever ghost is possessing Muggs has answers. Because until we know how to counter it, or how to exorcize these damned spirits, we're at a disadvantage."

"And there are more spirits coming," Annabelle said. "Isabelle feels it. They're coming for you. They want to take you like the rest."

I clenched my hands on my steering wheel. "Over my undead body."

Chapter 6

Back at the Underground, we had Muggs chained to a steel chair in our makeshift interrogation room. His wrists were bound with silver cuffs–enough to sting but not enough to burn. An hour or so later, he started to stir, his eyelids fluttering open. I was grateful that's as long as it took. We couldn't afford to waste any more of the night than was necessary. Once the sun rose I'd have to deal with inconveniences like kevlar suits or deadly sunburns. Then again, the sun might limit the possessed as much as it did me. So there was that. But did these ghosts understand the risks involved? What would happen to Mel and Juliet if the dumbasses possessing them decided to take a stroll outside in the middle of the day?

"Look who's awake," Pauli said, leaning against the wall, arms crossed. He gave me a wink, his rainbow scales shimmering in the dim light. "Ready for story time, bitch?"

Muggs' eyes opened fully, revealing a sickly green glow. Muggs was in there—but he wasn't the one we were facing. His gaze flitted between us, settling on Annabelle who stood behind me, her grip tight on Beli. The dragon-spirit dagger pulsed with brilliant energy, casting a verdant hue across the room.

"What is this?" The ghost in Muggs croaked, his voice layered with an echo that almost made it sound like it was coming from somewhere on the other side of the room. "You won't hurt me. Not really."

"Don't be so sure," I replied, stepping closer. "We're running out of patience, and you know what that means."

"Yes," the ghost inside Muggs sneered. "I know. This druid cares for you, Mercy. Like a daughter. And you, you care for him like he's your own child. A strange dynamic, really. Who's the parent in this relationship?"

"Shut up," I growled. "Tell me about this emperor. Who is possessing Mel? What are their plans?"

"Your threats are empty," the ghost continued, ignoring my question. "I'll tell you nothing. You'll do nothing to this vessel. You can't risk it. And if you do, what of it? I'll be free and I'll find the first vampire I can to take his place. Whoever might that be? I wonder..."

I shook my head. "This body's taken. Not available for residence."

"Is it, though? Where's that soul of yours?" the ghost asked. "Oh yes, it's not home. That means there's plenty of room in the Mercy Inn."

I rolled my eyes. "Your metaphors are lame."

The ghost cocked Muggs' eyebrow. "You ridicule my use of your language? Funny, since I only gained access to this Western tongue through my host's memories. I'm doing well, I should say, since it's my first day using English."

"Bravo, really," I said, my voice dripping with sarcasm. I had to wonder, though, if these ghosts could access enough of their hosts' memories to steal their language. What else did they know? Damn near everything, I was afraid. But I wasn't about to let my fear show. I had to maintain an air of confidence and control. It was the only way I'd get this ass clown to talk. "Your command of English is truly impressive. Now, tell me about the emperor or I'll make your existence here very uncomfortable."

"Empty threats, Mercy," the ghost inside Muggs taunted. "You won't harm this host. He means too much to you."

"She might not," Pauli chimed in, sliding up beside me with a grin that could only mean trouble. "But I don't know this old druid that well at all. Mercy, mind if I take a crack at this bitch?"

"Go ahead," I sighed, stepping back. Though letting Pauli take over anything made me mildly nervous. What, though, did we have to lose?

"Alright, here's the deal, sweetie," Pauli began, his voice silky-smooth. "I've got an expansive menu of delightful tortures, and trust me, you're gonna love them—or hate them. Depends on what you're in to. Either way, I'll have you begging... either to stop... or for more. And when you do, you'll tell me what we want to know."

"Please," the ghost scoffed. "You think such trivialities will break me?"

"Trivialities? Oh honey, I'm just warming up," Pauli said, winking at me. Then he turned back to Muggs... and dropped his pants. Using his shapeshifting abilities, he enhanced the size of his... you know what I'm talking about... until it was dragging on the floor. Then he picked it up and slapped Muggs right across the face with it like it was a rubber hose.

"What kind of perversion..." the ghost gagged. "Stop that!"

Pauli animated his... member... until it moved just like he did when he was a boa constrictor and wrapped it completely around Muggs' face. It might have been the most disturbing sight I'd ever seen—which is saying something. But it was so... grotesque... I couldn't help but watch at the same time.

"Say Uncle!" Pauli demanded.

The ghost responded with a muffled voice. I couldn't make out any of his words.

"I don't think he can breathe," Annabelle said. "Maybe loosen up a little?"

Pauli rolled his eyes. "Alright. But just for a second. If he doesn't talk..."

"Enough!" The ghost gasped for air the second Pauli gave him a chance to open his mouth. "You win. I'll talk. Just stop with your... whatever that thing is!"

"See? Was that so hard?" Pauli smirked triumphantly. "Actually it wasn't. It was flaccid. The hard torture comes next if you don't talk."

"No!" The ghost forced Muggs' face into an expression of genuine terror. I'd never seen the old man so afraid. "I told you I'll talk!"

"Then spill it," I demanded. "Who is possessing Mel?"

"Qin Shi Huang," the ghost finally admitted, his voice tinged with reluctant surrender. "The first emperor of China. His spirit inhabits Mel, seeking to revive his empire. But I already told you. He is coming for you, Mercy! Your progeny is just a means toward an end."

"Qin Shi Huang," I repeated, feeling the weight of ancient history settle over us. I knew little about his former reign, in his former life, but what little I knew was that he was a brutal ruler. From a long freaking time ago. The kind of leader who you wouldn't want commanding an army of ghost-possessed vampires. "And what are his plans?"

"He seeks to dominate the modern world, to establish his dynasty anew."

I glanced at Annabelle. All this, aside from the particular emperor's identity, was predictable. What else would an emperor who got a second shot at life chose to do with this newfound opportunity?

"Fine," Annabelle cut in, her voice sharp as the edge of her dragon-spirit dagger. "Now tell us about the magic he's using. How is it connected to the blood moon?"

The ghost in Muggs' body hesitated, eyes flickering with a sickly glow that made my skin crawl. "I don't know," he muttered finally, his voice trembling. "The emperor... he never told me how it's all connected."

"Don't give me that crap," I snarled, stepping closer until I could see the sweat beading on Muggs' forehead. "You expect us to believe you don't know? We've come too far for lies now. If you don't start talking, I'll turn you over to Pauli and let him have his fun. And trust me, you've seen *nothing* yet."

"Yeah, bitch," Pauli chimed in, voice dripping with glee. "I've got a *long* and *hard* list of ideas. None of them are family-friendly."

Muggs' face contorted into an expression of pure, abject horror. "Please! I swear on whatever soul I might still have left, I don't know the specifics of the magic! The emperor keeps many secrets. Even from his most trusted."

"You're lying," Annabelle accused, her eyes narrowing.

"I'm not!" Muggs' ghost cried, tears streaming down his cheeks. "The emperor himself isn't entirely sure how they came back. It's..." His voice broke, a sob catching in his throat. "It's someone else. Someone who orchestrated this. But the emperor doesn't know who it is."

"Great," I muttered, rolling my eyes. "So we've got some shadowy puppet master pulling strings behind the scenes. Fantastic."

"Regardless of who it is," the ghost continued, his voice shaky but insistent, "the emperor intends to seize this opportunity. He plans to force this nation to bend its knee to his empire. His Vampire Empire! It rhymes! Muahahaha!"

"Vampire Empire?" I scoffed, unable to keep the disdain out of my voice. "Seriously? That's the best he could come up with?"

"Has a ring to it, doesn't it?" A twisted grin spread across his face.

"You'll never manage. These vampires will not be the kind of army your emperor demands. You've seen it as much as I did. You feel it too. You people don't know how to use our bodies. The cravings are too much. An army requires discipline, and I've met toddlers with more control over their urges than you have."

"Discipline will come," the ghost retorted, eyes gleaming. "We will adjust. And when we do, you'll see just how formidable we can be."

"Adjust?" I snorted, a bitter laugh escaping my lips. "You're delusional if you think you can just 'adjust' to vampirism. It takes years. Decades. And some *never* adjust. Your emperor's poetry sucks, and so do his soldiers."

"They *literally suck!*" Pauli added. "Though not the way I'd hope. Nothing worse than when you're enjoying yourself and a boy gets his fangs involved."

I rolled my eyes and continued in on the ghost inside of Muggs. "You have no control. Your emperor's army is a bloodthirsty, chaotic brood, overwhelmed by cravings you don't understand."

"We are all our Highnesses' loyal subjects," the ghost in Muggs replied, his confidence unwavering. "We know discipline. We shall tame these urges of the flesh. And how much easier will it be once we have you in our ranks? You are their queen, are you not? You can command a great number of them, including this druid, with your bond."

"I'll never be *your* queen!" I spat. "I won't take part in your twisted empire. You'll never get me."

"Are you sure about that?" Muggs's eyes gleamed with a sickly light, the ghost's malice seeping through. "You were the emperor's initial target, but when you diverted his spirit with your magic, he chose the next-best option. A vampire you love as if she were your daughter. Will you not, when pressed, give yourself over to my emperor in exchange for your youngling's life?"

"Mel…" My heart clenched painfully at the mention of her name. The ghost knew exactly where to strike, exploiting the deepest vulnerability hidden beneath layers of defiance.

"Yes, Mel," the ghost hissed, savoring my reaction. "The emperor has her. She is his vessel now. You know what must be done to save her."

"You're bluffing," I said, though my voice wavered. "I won't fall for your mind games. We'll find another way to free her."

"Can you afford to take that chance?" he asked, his voice smooth and sinister. "Your magic might be powerful, Mercy, but is it enough? Even you have limits."

"Limits?" I sneered, masking my growing dread with bravado. "Your emperor really thinks he can use my progeny as leverage against me? Does he really think that will work?"

"Oh, it will work," the ghost was sounding more arrogant by the second. "Remember this: Love makes you vulnerable. It makes you weak."

"Get him out of my sight," I snarled, motioning for Pauli to take over. "Put him somewhere he can't escape."

"Happy to oblige," Pauli grinned, tossing his still oversized member over his shoulder. "Mind if I have a little more fun with him?"

I bit my lip. "I won't put Muggs through that. Sorry, Pauli."

Pauli shook his head—the one on his shoulders. Not the abnormally engorged head that belonged as much in a horror flick as an adult film. "You're such a Pauli pooper!"

As Pauli escorted the ghost away, that bastard's parting words lingered in the air like a sinister echo. They wanted *me*. Of course they did. What would they do to Mel, though, if I didn't turn myself over? How long would the emperor wait before he executed Mel and took off as a ghost again to come after me directly?

"What are we going to do?" Annabelle asked. "You can't turn yourself over to that bastard."

I shook my head. "I might not have a choice."

"You can't be serious," Annabelle said. "That won't solve anything."

I shrugged. "It could save Mel."

"For how long?" Annabelle huffed. "For all we know, another ghost will take her back all over again the first chance it gets."

I knew Annabelle was right. Sacrificing myself to the emperor wouldn't guarantee Mel's safety in the long run. It would only put me in his clutches, leaving my family vulnerable. I couldn't let that happen. The thought of Mel suffering because of me made my blood boil with a fierce determination to find another way.

"We need to think of a plan," I said, my mind racing through possibilities. "There has to be a way to free Mel without falling into their trap."

"We can't fight them all," Annabelle said. "Definitely not if you won't let me use Beli. I hate to say it, Mercy, but we might not have a choice."

I shook my head. "There's always a choice. Using Beli isn't an option. But we can use stakes. And wooden bullets. We have plenty of weaponry here in the armory."

"And only three of us to wield it all," Annabelle said. "I don't have all your super strength and speed, either. I can fight, and can handle myself against a vampire or three, but against that many? We need help, Mercy."

"No vampires," I sighed. "So calling up Hailey again is out of the question. I might know someone who'd be willing to help. If he and his partner are in the area—which is a big if."

Annabelle tilted her head. "A werewolf? A warlock? Who is it?"

I smirked. "His name's Sebastian. And he's the only hunter I've ever met who bested *me* and lived to tell about it."

"You really think this is a good idea?" Annabelle asked. "You said he *bested* you? Bested you how? He staked you?"

"We won't go into that. But he also saved my life from Oblivion. The first time I had to deal with that scaly bastard."

Annabelle tilted her head. "Heard about that. Sorry that happened."

I shook my head. "Ever been with a man who makes you feel like you don't exist? Well, with Oblivion, that's precisely what he wanted. But not just for me. For everyone. The son of a bitch got off on non-existence."

Annabelle looked at me with wide eyes. Sympathetic eyes. Gross. "Wish you would have asked me to help, then. Beli has his opinions about Oblivion. Intel you could have used."

I chuckled. "Yeah, sorry. Didn't think about it. No offense, but you're usually the last person I think to call in circumstances like this."

"Then why'd you call me now?"

"Truth?" I laughed a little. "I was just hoping to get Isabelle. But if you had to come with her as a package deal, so be it."

Annabelle rolled her eyes. "Well, you have a habit of turning enemies into allies, Mercy. I'm here to help, along with Isabelle, whether or not you want me. And if this Sebastian guy is as good as you say he is, I say you call him."

Chapter 7

The entire Underground shook, dust falling from the ceiling like powdered sugar on a beignet. Annabelle's eyes widened in alarm, her eyes pulsing green for a moment, signaling Isabelle's alarm.

"Relax," I said with a chuckle, leaning casually against the damp stone wall. "That's just Sebastian's ride. Some kind of muscle car, a Chevelle, I think."

"You're kidding me.," Annabelle cocked an eyebrow. "I thought this guy was a monster hunter. How can a hunter hope to sneak up on his prey if his car registers on the Richter scale?"

"Sebastian doesn't worry about the element of surprise." I pushed off the wall and started walking toward the elevator. "He'd rather strike fear into those he's hunting. He doesn't mind announcing his arrival. If they're afraid, they're careless. That's his philosophy, anyway."

"How good can this guy really be?" Annabelle asked, a crooked grin and raised eyebrow betraying her skepticism. "You said he has no powers?"

"None," I confirmed, pressing the button for the elevator.

"Doesn't use any magic?" she pressed further, clearly not convinced.

"Not really," I said, stepping into the elevator as it arrived with a clank. "He has a few enchanted items, but mostly, it's all about skill and determination. And trust me, he's got plenty of both."

"Skill and determination, huh?" Annabelle stepped into the elevator beside me. "Sounds like a load of bullshit."

"Well, you'll see soon enough." I pressed the button that would take us topside. "And Pauli, try not to drool?"

"Don't drool?" Pauli tilted his head. "Is he..."

I laughed. "You'll see."

The elevator doors parted, and I stepped out into the garage, Pauli and Annabelle following close behind.

And there it was on the curb just outside our garage: Sebastian's 1970 cherry-red Chevelle with black racing stripes, purring like an apex predator waiting to strike.

Sebastian and Donnie stepped out of their car as soon as they saw us.

"Dayum!" Pauli fanned himself theatrically. "I think I've died and gone to hunk heaven!"

"Is that Jason Momoa?" Annabelle's jaw was half-way to the floor.

"Eat your hearts out, you two. He's not *available*. Been searching for his wife for the last decade. After she was abducted by some kind of monster he has yet to find."

"Why doesn't he move on?" Annabelle asked, crossing her arms. Her curiosity was piqued, but she tried to mask it with a veneer of indifference. "After a decade? What are the chances she's still alive? Most monsters don't abduct people so they can keep them around for small talk."

"Because he's in love," I said with a sigh. I was happy with Juliet, now, but when I first met Sebastian, I felt the same way. If I were ever interested in a *mortal*, for anything other than a snack, he'd be the one. "Besides, why are you so interested? Aren't you still with that voodoo demigod?"

"Ogoun, the Loa of War." Annabelle flipped her hair over her shoulder. "Romance with a demigod isn't everything a lot of paranormal authors out there would like you to think. Thrilling, for a time, but they aren't exactly monogamous as a matter of habit."

"Does it matter?" I asked.

"To me, sure it does. I might be the Voodoo Queen, but I'm still a Catholic girl. Just like Marie Laveau was before me. I have standards. We tried that whole open relationship thing for a while. He loved it, obviously. Wasn't for me."

I cocked an eyebrow. "What did you expect? Did you really think a demigod was going to settle down with you and start a family?"

Annabelle sighed. "I was young and naïve. I don't know what I expected. You don't always think things through when you're blinded by what you think is love. He's still a part of our world, of course. And we get along well enough. But we want different things."

Finally, Sebastian and Donnie approached. A welcome intrusion on our conversation. The last thing I wanted to do was play the girlfriend role to Annabelle Mulledy. But I did understand how being a part of the supernatural world could complicate relationships. I'd say I empathized with her but… pssshhh… I'm Mercy Brown. I'd never admit to empathizing with anyone.

Sebastian and Donnie approached. They reminded me of Arnold Schwarzenegger and Danny DeVito in Twins. An odd paring, to say the least. Sebastian Winter was a genuine lady-killer, but had no interest in anyone who wasn't his long-lost bride. Donnie was probably a real-life forty-year-old virgin, but thought he was God's gift to women. Which might have been true if he belonged to a community of hobbits.

Donnie puffed out his chest like a peacock in full display, trying to catch Annabelle's eye. The problem? Donnie's moobs weren't exactly as impressive as a plume of multi-colored feathers. It took everything in me not to laugh; the guy had the physique of the Pillsbury Doughboy but when he looked in the mirror all he saw was Hulk Hogan in his prime.

"Sebastian." I nodded.

"Mercy," he acknowledged with a curt bob of his head in kind. He glanced at Annabelle and Pauli.

"These are my friends," I introduced them. "Annabelle, Pauli, meet Sebastian and Donnie."

Pauli's eyes sparkled with mischief as he sized up Sebastian, while Annabelle couldn't take her eyes off him. Neither of them gave Donnie so much as a glance—but he didn't care. Annabelle was captivated by him.

Good Lord, I thought to myself. This was going to get annoying fast. We had ghosts to exorcise from my friends. The last thing I was in the mood to put up with was a middle-school crush betwixt my mortal friends.

"Pleasure to meet you both," Sebastian said, extending a hand to shake.

"Likewise," Annabelle replied, short of breath.

"Well, damn, Sebastian, I'm surprised you got here so quickly." I said, trying to push past awkward introductions. "I figured you'd be half-way across the country tracking something nasty."

"We were already in the area," Sebastian said, shaking his head. "Given what's going on out there, this is nasty central at the moment."

"Speaking of which," he said, scrutinizing me closely. "I was a little surprised you called. I figured you'd been taken like the rest. I don't see any strange glow from your eyes. But how can I know for sure you're still you, and not possessed like every other vampire we've come across?"

I rolled my eyes. "Kiss my dead ass, Sebas."

"Yup, still the same Mercy," he laughed.

"Damn straight."

"Should have known that you of all vampires would avoid all this." He shook his head again, this time with a hint of admiration.

I took a deep breath—not because I required oxygen, but out of exacerbation. "It's a small miracle. But they got my entire team. Mel and Muggs, and my new girlfriend, Juliet."

Sebastian's left eyebrow rose slightly. He didn't know about Juliet, but he said nothing. He didn't strike me as the kind of person to care one way or another who fell for who. I couldn't blame him for being surprised, though. Falling for Juliet had shocked me more than anyone. I didn't *historically* swing that way, but when blood-bonds and magic are involved, passion can get its initial spark in ways you'd never expect.

And sometimes all it takes is a spark to ignite a flame.

"Come on in," I said, turning on my heel, back toward the elevator. "We've got a lot to cover. Intelligence to share.

And we need to arm up. There's no telling how long it'll be before this... condition spreads."

"Until it spreads?" Sebastian's voice was gruff behind me. "A little late for that."

I stopped in my tracks. "Say what?"

"This is ground zero, Mercy. That's why we're in tow. But I've had reports of vampires suffering similar conditions half-way across the country over just a few hours."

Annabelle gasped, her usual bravado faltering for a moment. "New Orleans, too?"

"Last we heard, yeah. Especially New Orleans." Sebastian's tone carried the weight of bad news he didn't enjoy delivering.

"Shit," Annabelle muttered under her breath. She sighed heavily, her shoulders slumping just a bit.

I bit my lip. "Do you need to go back there? Check things out? There are more vampires in New Orleans than Rhode Island."

Annabelle shook her head. "New Orleans isn't just a hub for vampires. There are other supernaturals, allies, there who can rise to the occasion. I imagine Hailey's managing to resist just as you did. Not to mention all of Vilokan. But the emperor, the leader of these ghost-possessed vamps, is here. Like Sebastian said, this is ground zero. If this is going to be stopped everywhere, we have to stop it here first."

"Good," I nodded, satisfied, and pressed my hand to the palm-reader that opened the elevator. "Then let's get to work."

The elevator doors opened with a soft ping, and we all shuffled inside. The metallic walls of the elevator gleamed under the fluorescent lights, reflecting our tense faces back at us.

Donnie sauntered in, trying to exude casual confidence as he propped himself against the wall. He gave Annabelle a sly side glance and flashed his best attempt at a charming smile. "You have Wi-Fi here?"

He wasn't looking at me, but I was the best one to answer. "Yeah, but I don't know the password. Why are you asking?"

Donnie's eyes were fixed directly on Annabelle's chest. "Because I'm feeling a strong connection."

I snorted.

Annabelle didn't even bother to look up from her phone, her fingers tapping out a rapid message. She was probably checking in with her contacts in New Orleans about the status of the vampire-ghost situation there. "Dream on, pal." she replied without so much as raising her eyes from her screen.

Sebastian chuckled deeply, his laughter echoing in the confined space. "Nice try, Donnie. You might want to save those lines for the girls on Fortnite."

"Tried that," Donnie huffed. "Most of the girls on there are actually dudes. Learned that the hard way."

I clasped my hand over my mouth to stifle a laugh.

Donnie continued. "Women these days just don't appreciate the finer things. They're all about burgers and fries. I'm a filet mignon."

"More like a rump roast." I couldn't help but snort through the chortle that escaped my hand.

Pauli squeezed Donnie's shoulder. "I know how you feel. I'm into the finest meats myself. How do you feel about *kielbasa*, honey?"

Donnie gasped as if Pauli's comment sucked the air right out of his lungs. "I, uhh... not really my favorite..."

Pauli traced his finger around Donnie's jaw-line. "I'll butter your rolls any time. And you know what goes great with rolls, right? A great, big pen—"

The elevator dinged just in time. "Alright, everyone! Let's stick to the mission at hand, shall we?"

"At hand?" Pauli tilted his head. "If that's what Donnie-bear here wants... but I'm more a sucker than a stroker."

Donnie screeched and took off running down the hall. Everyone else burst out laughing.

"Thanks for deflecting, Pauli." Annabelle chuckled.

"You think I did that for you?" Pauli shook his head. "Alright, maybe I did. But I meant every word. I'm a man who appreciates variety. I can appreciate a little jiggle with my wiggle."

Chapter 8

"Excuse the mess," I said, gesturing at the wreckage of what used to be my throne room. "I had a bit of an... outburst after finding out my entire team was forcibly drafted into a ghost army."

"Understandable," Sebastian responded dryly, settling himself on one of the couches I hadn't demolished.

"We need to get everything we've each learned out on the table," I continued, locking eyes with Sebastian. "We managed to capture Muggs. He's like the rest—possessed. But we got some intel from the ghost rattling around in his swollen dome. The leader possessing Mel is none other than Emperor Qin Shi Huang. You know, the first emperor of China. Real piece of work. I need to do more research, haven't had the chance, and we only just learned all of this. But what we know is that the emperor was obsessed with immortality. Killed many people in his time."

"He also told us that the emperor is planning to do what emperors do," Annabelle added. "Expand his empire. Conquer people. And he's going to use vampires possessed by the ghosts of his ancient army to do it."

"Basically," Pauli piped up. "This emperor is a real bitch."

"Right," I chuckled a little. "The thing is, the ghost in Muggs didn't know the specific magic used to bring the Emperor and his warriors back. Even the emperor isn't sure how the magic works. There's someone else responsible for all of this. Someone with a vested interest in bringing China's first emperor back."

"Interesting," Sebastian mused, fingers steepled under his chin. "I've been tracing a lead on the spell responsible for this mess. And here's where it gets real spicy—this isn't some random supernatural chaos. It's political. An orchestrated effort by interests in China to either overthrow the United States completely or, at the very least, sow enough chaos to cripple us."

"Wait, what?" Annabelle's eyes widened. "You're seriously saying this is an attack by the Chinese government?"

"I don't know if the actual government is involved or not," Sebastian nodded. "But you know how things like this are. Shadow organizations. Non-government organizations doing the government's bidding. There's no way to trace all this crap down from here. But if I were a betting man, I'd wager using the spirit of a dead emperor with an expansionist agenda wasn't a mistake. Whoever's behind this might be content if all that resulted was chaos, but they certainly hoped for more—that this vampire-ghost army would conquer the United States from within."

"Are you serious right now?" I snapped. "You already knew all this shit and didn't call me up? You already knew everything we found out about the emperor that took over Mel?"

Sebastian shrugged nonchalantly. "I assumed you were taken by the ghosts like the rest of the vampires we've encountered. Look, like I said, this isn't the Chinese government. Not officially. There's an organization that might be involved, something with ties to Emperor Qin Shi Huang that goes all the way back to the times of his Terracotta Army."

"Forgive me for my lack of knowledge about the history of all this," Annabelle said. "We've been literally chasing ghosts all night and haven't had the time to do much more than a basic Google search. Wikipedia told us a couple things. Qin Shi Huang died in 210 BC, right?"

"Yes," Donnie added. "Whatever organization is involved is *at least* that old. Probably was established at some point during the emperor's dynasty."

"Great, just great," I muttered, running a hand through my tangled hair. "So, we're dealing with a bunch of ancient ghost whisperers with a modern day political agenda to boot?"

"Seems that way," Sebastian conceded. "But we need to focus on the task at hand. If we can figure out how they did the ritual, we might be able to reverse it."

I folded my arms over my chest. "Do you have any specific leads on this society, or whoever they are, or are we just flailing around in the dark here?"

"Calm down, Mercy," Sebastian replied, rubbing his temples as if he were dealing with a particularly annoying child. "Donnie's got information that might help."

I threw my arms in the air. "Alright, Donnie Darko. Enlighten us, would you?"

"Good movie," Donnie said. "But my last name is Levingston."

I stared at Donnie blankly. The kind of look that said, "Cut the shit, or I'll have you for dessert."

Donnie cleared his throat. "Sorry. Not...the...point..."

"Come on, Donnie," Annabelle said. "Just tell us what you know."

Donnie blushed a little—not just on his cheeks, but on the crown of his shiny bald head. Just because Annabelle *acknowledged* his existence. The guy really was smitten by the voodoo queen. He cleared his throat and adjusted his glasses. "The Blood Rite of the Terracotta Warriors is some heavy-duty necromancy. It's not just about raising spirits; because using lunar magic in necromantic rites is common. But *controlling* it, namely, dictating which specific spirits might be raised, gets trickier."

"I know all about necromancy," Annabelle piped in. "I've dealt with my share of nasty caplatas who've used power like that to animate the dead before. Standard bad-girl Voodoo. Nothing like this, though."

Donnie extended his finger as if to make a point. "Right! Of course! But what's different is this ancient Chinese magic. You see, in China, ancestor worship was always a thing. You ever read Harry Potter?"

I rolled my eyes. "Get to the fucking point, Donnie!"

"The horcruxes. How Voldemort split up his soul and put parts of it in different objects. This Terracotta blood rite is similar."

"So we have to go horcrux hunting now?" I asked. "Isn't that lovely?"

"Not exactly," Donnie said. "But sort of, yeah. As you already mentioned, Emperor Qin Shi Huang was *obsessed* with living forever. He searched for years for an elixir that would grant him immortality. Every attempt was a failure. But then he learned about a wizard, Anqi Sheng, who was *already* a thousand years old then! The emperor set out for Mount Pengali, where the wizard was rumored to live. Legend has it that the emperor spent three days in conversation with the immortal wizard. Mysteriously, the emperor seemed to give up his quest for immortality after that."

"Just gave up?" I asked.

Donnie grinned widely. "He *seemed* to. No more quests. No experimental elixirs. There's a belief that the emperor got the answer he sought. A way to *achieve* immortality, but without the means to actually accomplish it. The emperor began making all the preparations to revive himself and his army some day—once the means became viable again."

"The means?" Annabelle asked.

Donnie nodded. "The wizard, Anqi Sheng, told the emperor how to cast a part of his soul into something that might endure. The rite itself would make the object that contains the spell immortal. But there were no longer any *living* beings who walked the earth at that time, with the fortitude to survive the spell."

"And there were at the time the ancient wizard became immortal himself?" I asked.

Donnie shook his head. "No one knows for sure. Perhaps it was an ancient vampire, an offspring of your sire, Niccolo the Damned. But I think you can see where this is going..."

"That's why they're using vampires." I was pacing now but didn't even remember starting to. "We're the vessels that can survive the spell. The blood moon magic, the rite, extracts the souls from whatever inanimate objects the emperor and his Terracotta Warriors used as temporary vessels and frees them to find bodies that are formidable enough to survive the magic."

"Bingo!" Donnie said. "Here's the thing, though. It takes time for this kind of magic to work. Until the ghosts, the souls of the Terracotta Warriors and the Emperor, fully integrate with their new bodies, a part of their essence still lingers in whatever vessel they've survived in all these thousands of years."

Sebastian locked eyes with me. I stopped pacing. "We think that if we can find these vessels, whatever they are, and destroy them, it might also eliminate the ghosts inhabiting your friends."

"But you said whatever these souls go into becomes indestructible."

"There's always a loophole," Annabelle added. "Anything can be destroyed with the right method or magic. We just have to figure it out."

Pauli raised his hand. "Can I ask a question?"

I rolled my eyes, expecting some kind of lewd joke. "Go ahead, Pauli."

"Serious question. Aren't vampires already invulnerable? Sunlight and wooden stakes aside. What will happen when the magic of these souls fully merges with these vampire bodies?"

"My best guess?" Sebastian added. "The usual vampire vulnerabilities won't affect them. They'll be daywalkers. Stakes won't penetrate the heart."

I gasped. "They'll be unstoppable. And my friends..."

"Lost," Donnie said. "Trapped as eternal prisoners in their bodies, at the mercy of the Terracotta Warriors who took them over."

"How much time do we have?" Annabelle asked. "Before these spirits fully integrate with their vampire hosts?"

"Your guess is as good as mine," Donnie said. "What I know about all of this is piece-meal from a dozen different sources. Most of it from Reddit forums. The information I have isn't exactly top-notch credible."

"It's something." I shook my head. "Better than what we had before. We have to assume the worst. That the merger of ancient spirits with vampires is imminent."

"Which means finding whatever relics or objects we need to destroy to annihilate these ghosts." Annabelle sighed. "Any idea at all where to look?"

"Actually, yes," Sebastian interjected, leaning forward with a glint in his eye. "Since Providence is the epicenter of this... blood moon situation... someone must have performed whatever blood rite was done somewhere in the region.

"Well, don't leave us hanging," I snapped, trying to keep my frustration in check. "Where exactly?"

"Chinatown," Donnie said. "As good a place to start as any."

I tilted my head. "Chinatown went under decades ago. The whole area was demolished back in the sixties. But back when I was a girl there *was* a Chinatown in providence. Ironically enough, it was on Empire Street."

"You really think that's a coincidence?" Annabelle asked. "Empire Street? The center of old Chinatown?"

I shook my head. "I don't believe in coincidences. Chinatown might be long gone, but I'd bet anything that what we're looking for is there. Somewhere."

Chapter 9

As the SUV rolled to a stop on Empire Street, I glanced out the window and took in the eerie stillness. The once-bustling heart of Chinatown had been reduced to empty buildings and cracked sidewalks. An urban renewal project had forced the Chinese community to scatter more than sixty years ago. At least that's what I learned from a quick Google search of Chinatown in Providence. The last I knew, as a girl, it was a thriving community of immigrants. But I hadn't been to Providence since becoming a vampire. It was hardly the same city, in any respect, that it was back then.

"Alright, let's get this party started." I opened the door and stepped out, my boots crunching against the remnants of a broken beer bottle left in the street. Annabelle slid out from the passenger seat and slammed the door shut. Pauli got out from the back and sashayed over to Annabelle's side.

"Shut up, Pauli," I snapped, though a ghost of a smile touched my lips.

Sebastian's Chevelle pulled up next to us, its engine growling loud enough to wake the whole damn neighborhood before silencing. Sebastian got out first, followed by Donnie, who tried and failed to suppress a yawn as he made his way toward us.

"Humans," I chuckled under my breath. "What's the matter Donnie boy? Getting a little sleepy?"

Donnie grunted. "Look, I don't look this good by skipping my beauty rest."

"Sure you don't."

Donnie tossed something at Annabelle and she caught it.

"What the—"

It was a bag of chips. Annabelle glanced at the bag and scoffed as she examined the Lays logo on the front. "*Let me guess*. You were going to tell me I just got Lay-d by Donnie."

"Damn!" Donnie huffed. "How'd you know that was the line I was about to use? I've been saving that one for a special someone!"

Annabelle rolled her eyes and tossed the chips back at him. "I'm more of a Doritos girl. Like my father used to be when I was little. A *chip* off the old block, you know."

I glared at Annabelle. "That's the worst dad joke I've ever heard."

"I tried," Annabelle said. "What can I say? I'm not a Dad."

"We could always share a can of Pringles," Donnie piped up. "Once you pop, pop, pop!" He made a thrusting motion with his hips. "You can't stop!"

Annabelle and I stared at him blankly for what felt like a good minute—it was really just a second or two. Neither of us had a response. Some comments are best left ignored.

I did a quick survey of our surroundings. The streets were eerily silent, every shadow and corner imbued with an unsettling stillness. It was 3:00 a.m., prime witching hour so far as spirits were concerned, but the emptiness was to be expected. There could be a few rogue ghosts still out and about that hadn't found hosts yet, so I had to stay on my guard. The last thing I wanted was to become a skin-suit for a member of the Terracotta Army.

"Alright," Sebastian said, scanning the area. "If this is 'ground zero' for the blood moon ritual, then there should be ghost-possessed vampires lurking about. If our theory is accurate, and there are some relics of some kind that protect these spirits, there's bound to be a vampire or twenty standing guard."

"We could split up to look for clues," Sebastian suggested. "Cover more ground in less time."

I raised my hand and sniffed at the air.

Sebastian shot me a curious look. "What are you doing?"

"These ghosts don't know how to handle their vampiric cravings." I paused, ensuring everyone was paying attention. "That means, if there are any in the neighborhood, there's been blood spilled nearby. I should be able to smell it."

"Good thinking." Sebastian crossed his arms and kicked at a loose piece of grave on the street. "Picking up anything?"

"Not yet," I replied. "But it's hard to remember exactly where on Empire St. Chinatown used to be. I barely remember it all, much less can place it based on today's landmarks. If we get close to any vampires who've fed as of late, I'll know."

"Mel in the area?" Annabelle asked.

I shook my head. "She's on the move around the outskirts of the city. I can sense her out there. But she's not in this neighborhood."

Suddenly, a blood-curdling scream pierced the silence, sending a jolt of adrenaline through my veins. "Pauli, help everyone catch up," I barked, my instincts taking over. Without waiting for a response, I propelled myself forward with vampiric speed, my surroundings blurring past me.

I arrived at an alleyway within seconds, skidding to a halt as I took in the sight before me. A homeless woman lay crumpled on the ground, her neck marred by twin puncture wounds. Fresh blood trickled slowly from the bites, pooling underneath her limp form.

"Shit," I muttered under my breath, crouching beside her. Her pulse was faint, but she was still alive—for now.

A flash of rainbow light illuminated the alley, and the rest of the team materialized beside me, wrapped together by Pauli's serpentine form. He unwound himself with a flourish, grinning broadly. "That's how you do it. Three at the same time. My specialty. Though usually my foursomes don't include a girl."

Annabelle shook her head, a smirk playing on her lips. "You couldn't handle one of me, honey. Even if you wanted to."

"Please, baby Belle," Pauli retorted, winking theatrically. "I can handle what I want, but as fabulous as you are, you just aren't my type."

"Focus, people," I snapped, rising to my feet and scanning the alley for any immediate threats. The air was thick with the metallic scent of blood, mingling with the stench of decay and desperation that clung to every shadowed corner.

"Is she going to make it?" Annabelle asked, her voice softer now as she knelt beside the woman, her hand hovering uncertainly.

"Hard to say," I admitted, glancing back at Sebastian. "We need to find out who did this. They can't have gone far. I ran here as fast as I could. They must've heard me coming and took off mid-feed."

"Hold up," Sebastian said suddenly, raising his fist to silence everyone. His eyes were fixed on some distant point in the darkness.

"What's up?" Pauli asked.

"Shh," Sebastian hissed, tilting his head slightly, listening intently. I strained my senses, trying to catch whatever he had detected. The faintest rustle, a whisper of movement—how had he picked that up with his human senses?

Sebastian took off running without another word.

"Dammit," I cursed under my breath, sprinting after him. My vampiric speed made closing the distance easy, but I couldn't help but marvel at how swiftly he moved. So far as humans went, he was an extraordinary specimen.

Sebastian rounded a corner just as I caught up, and I saw him whip out a long silver chain from his pocket, swinging it deftly. The chain struck something solid with a metallic clang, followed by a surprised yelp.

"Nice move," I said between breaths, reaching his side just in time to see the figure he had taken down.

Pink hair spilled across the ground like a neon waterfall. My heart lurched. "Juliet!" I gasped, dropping to my knees beside her. Her eyes were wild, unfocused, and glowed with the trademark green that haunted the eyes of all the possessed.

"You know this vampire?" Sebastian still held the chain taut around her neck.

"That's Juliet. My girlfriend." My voice was barely a whisper.

"Mercy, that might be Juliet's locomotive, but she's not the conductor," Donnie cautioned. "Don't get too close. These spirits might be able to jump bodies."

"He's right," Sebastian added, wincing slightly as Juliet—technically whoever was inhabiting her—struggled against the silver. "Best keep your distance. Just in case."

"Juliet, can you hear me?" I called as I looked at her from a distance.

"She can hear you," an unfamiliar voice choked out. "Why don't you come over here and give me a kiss?"

"Like hell I will," I spat back, my fangs elongating with a hiss. The possessive spirit within Juliet cackled, a grotesque sound that sent shivers down my spine. Despite the danger, I couldn't help but feel a pang of sorrow at the sight of Juliet's body being used like that. The same body I knew, I caressed, I kissed... now the mere shell for an ancient spirit.

Sebastian tightened his grip on the silver chain, his jaw set in determination. "Who are you, what are you protecting here?"

"I'm protecting nothing! Just out for a bite..." It was Juliet's face, but the expressions that dressed her countenance were a stranger's. It barely even looked like her anymore.

"You don't have to talk," Sebastian said, glancing back from the direction we came. "You headed down this alley. A dead-end. You wouldn't come down *here* unless you were trying to retreat to protect what you're guarding."

"You think you know so much, human! I tell you the truth, you will soon bow before the great dynasty of Qin Shi Huang!"

Sebastian chuckled and glanced at me briefly. "Why do the bad guys always have so much *bravado*?"

"I know, right!" I laughed. "But I see where you're going with your reasoning. That door at the end of the alley. It's cracked open. I can see it through the darkness, just as if it were the day."

Sebastian nodded but held the chain tight around Juliet's neck. "What you're protecting is inside, isn't it?"

"Nothing is in there at all!" Juliet's lips curled, and the laughter that came out of them wasn't like any she'd ever make. "I just made a... wrong turn... silly me. What you're looking for, it's the *other* direction! I'll take you to it, I will!"

"Through the door then?" Sebastian winked at me.

I nodded. "Let's go."

Chapter 10

The alley was a narrow strip of darkness, the kind that threatened to swallow you whole if you lingered too long. I glanced at Juliet—well, the ghost riding shotgun in Juliet's body. A surge of irritation burned like acid in my veins.

"Pauli," I said, my voice low and commanding, "take Juliet back to a cell in the Underground. There's a vacant one next to where we're holding Muggs. Drop her off there."

"You wouldn't!" The ghost's voice twisted Juliet's features into something unrecognizable, a grotesque mask of indignation. "You cannot imprison me! I am the Emperor's most loyal subject! When he hears of this, he will avenge me, I say! He'll avenge me!"

"Can't imprison you?" I huffed. "Tell that to my girlfriend, asshole." I glared at the ghost through Juliet's eyes with every ounce of vampiric menace I could muster.

"Right-o, boss lady." With a quick flicker of colorful light, Pauli appeared on Juliet's shoulders, curled the back part of his body around the silver chain binding her, and wound himself around her. Another flash, and they were gone.

I wasn't sure if I was relieved we had Juliet or more worried about her. What could this ghost do to her in retaliation for locking it up? The ghost possessing Muggs had made threats before. So far, it had done nothing to him. That didn't mean that either Muggs or Juliet were safe, though. But it was a slight relief to know I knew where they were.

I barely had time to process my conflicted emotions over the encounter I'd had with the ghost inside Juliet when another flash of rainbow light signaled Pauli's return.

"She's all locked up," Pauli announced, still in snake form, dropping himself right over my shoulders.

I shuddered. "Get off! I'm not your ride!"

Pauli giggled a little, then flashed again and appeared back on Annabelle's shoulders. She stroked his head gently as if he were her pet—what a strange friendship those two had.

"What we're looking for is probably inside," Sebastian said, casting a wary glance toward the door at the end of the alley. "But we have no idea what we're walking into."

"I might pick up a few things," I said, focusing my enhanced hearing. It took several years before I could direct my ears like that. A vampire's senses can be overwhelming to younglings. Over time, though, most of us adjust and learn to shut things out. By silencing what I didn't want to hear, I could focus on whatever might be lurking inside the strange door. It was oddly quiet inside, but there were entities inside. What kind of entities? I wasn't a hundred percent sure.

Whoever they were, they weren't especially talkative. I didn't pick up a single spoken word. Just motion. Shuffling. Eerie as hell.

"Well?" Annabelle asked, her fingers twitching nervously by the hilt of her dagger.

"Quiet. Too quiet," I replied, straining to catch more details. "There are people—more likely, vampires—in there. But it's strange how silent they are."

"How many are we talking about?" Annabelle pressed, her eyes narrowing as she peered into the darkness.

"Too difficult to tell," I said, shaking my head. "But they're definitely vampires. Otherwise, I'd hear more heartbeats."

"No heartbeats means no humans at least," Annabelle added, a hint of relief in her voice. "Less carnage than before."

"Not necessarily," I countered, giving her a grim look. "No heartbeats just means the vampires in there are done with dinner."

"Great." Sebastian rubbed his right temple. "Can you smell blood?"

"Yeah," I said, inhaling deeply and letting the myriad scents flow over me. "It's in the air, but subtle. Not coming from near the door. Also, the shuffling I'm hearing is muffled, but there's also an echo. It's like the sound is coming through a long tunnel or something."

"Perfect," he sighed, reaching into his bag and pulling out a pair of sleek glasses. Donnie pulled out a pair from his jacket pocket as well.

"Night vision," Donnie explained, slipping them on and adjusting them. He pulled out another set and tossed them to Annabelle.

"Thanks," she said, donning the glasses. "These should help."

"Hey, what about me?" Pauli hissed, his forked-tongue flickering.

"Boa constrictors are nocturnal," Annabelle said. "You'll be fine. Just stay in this form."

Pauli slithered under Annabelle's arms and over her shoulders, his scales shimmering faintly even in the dim light. Better her than me.

Donnie took up the rear. He had a few throwing knives in his belt. He knew how to use them, too. A lot of years in his mother's basement throwing them at posters of who knows what had refined his skill. You wouldn't know it by looking at him, but he was a decent fighter, all things considered. He was no Sebastian, but he could hold his own.

We stepped into the dark room, our footsteps echoing off the dusty floor. It looked like nothing remarkable at first glance—just another abandoned space that had seen better days. Dust hung in the air, particles catching the faint beams of light that shone in from the streetlights through dirty windows.

"Looks like nobody's home," Annabelle whispered.

"Doubt that's the case. You said it sounded like the noises were echoing through a tunnel?"

I nodded and pressed through a door barely hanging on its hinges. Through it, a steep stone staircase descended into darkness.

"Ah, there we go." Sebastian stepped through first. "Down we go, then."

"Wait," Annabelle said, her hand gripping Pauli's serpentine form tightly. "A small stairway like this. If there are vampires out and about and they come at us from behind, and still more meet us from below, they could catch us in an ambush."

"Good thinking. Pauli?"

"I'll be ready," Pauli said. "I can get us out of here in a flash if it comes to that."

"Remember," I added, giving Annabelle a sharp look. "Wooden stakes are alright if necessary. Try to avoid using Beli unless there's no other choice."

"Understood," Annabelle nodded, her expression serious. She knew as well as I did that unleashing Beli wasn't totally off the table. If push came to shove and we had no other choice, she could use it. And with Muggs and Juliet secured, I didn't have to worry about *them* being consigned straight to hell. Didn't mean I wanted to see *any* of my team suffer that kind of fate.

And Mel was still somewhere *out there*. Moving at a distance. She wasn't where we were going.

Donnie retrieved a wooden stake from his backpack and handed it to Annabelle. "Just in case you need it."

Annabelle took the stake, twirling it between her fingers before slipping it through a loop in her belt. "Thanks."

"Let's move," I said, and we began our descent down the stone staircase. The air grew dank and musty, the scent of blood becoming stronger with each step. The walls closed in around us, like we were navigating the bowels of some kind of stone monster.

"Dammit!" I cursed as I walked straight into a sticky spider web, the fine strands clinging to my face and hair. I hastily brushed them away, feeling a shiver crawl down my spine.

"Watch your step," Sebastian said dryly, his gauntlet-clad hand pushing aside some of the webbing. "If there's a web here, one of two things is most likely. Either whoever is down here in these catacombs has been here a while. A spider doesn't take long to spin a new web, but we can safely assume there haven't been a lot of people coming and going for a few hours at least."

"You said it's one of two possibilities?" I asked.

"Or there's another way in and out of this place," Sebastian said. "Other than this staircase."

"Great," I muttered, stepping carefully forward. The musty smell mixed with the iron tang of blood grew sharper, stinging my nostrils. "Just what we need. More surprises."

Annabelle sighed. "This place goes almost as deep as the stairway into Vilokan in New Orleans." She paused, her brows knitting together. "You don't build a staircase going down this deep into the earth if you don't have something big down there, something worth hiding."

"Yeah," I said, feeling a cool draft on my face. "I can feel the air flowing out from below. There's definitely a large expanse down there."

"Could this be where old Chinatown went?" Sebastian asked, his voice echoing slightly in the confined space.

"Hold up!" Annabelle suddenly grabbed my arm, her grip surprisingly strong.

"What is it?" I asked, peering into the darkness ahead.

"Do you feel that?" she whispered, cocking her head as if her ears were antennas trying to pick up a faint signal.

"Feel what?" I asked.

"It's a magic. Something familiar." Then her eyes widened with surprise. "Too familiar. It can't be..."

"Voodoo?" I asked. I didn't sense it myself, but that was the kind of magic Annabelle knew. it was a reasonable deduction.

Annabelle nodded. "Has to be."

"Voodoo? In old Chinatown?" Sebastian sounded skeptical. "Isn't Voodoo of African origins?"

"Lines aren't so neatly drawn as they used to be." Annabelle shook her head. "People mix practices all the time."

"Agreed," I added. "A lot of modern practitioners mix and match their arts. They're eclectic. Which can be extremely dangerous when they don't know what they're doing."

"Fantastic," Pauli said, his snake eyes gleaming in the dim light. "So, we're dealing with a bunch of amateur dead vampires screwing with magic they don't understand. What could go wrong?"

"Stay sharp," I warned, gripping my wand tighter. "We don't know what kind of twisted spell craft we might run into next."

As we descended further, the air grew cooler and more damp. The scent of mold mixed with blood. We finally reached the bottom of the stairs, and I couldn't help but gasp at the sight before us.

"Chinese architecture," Sebastian murmured, his voice filled with awe. "This has been here a long time. I don't think they're building like this in Beijing these days."

We examined the ancient underground city all around us. Stone arches and intricately carved pillars stretched out into the darkness, illuminated only by oil lamplight and the occasional flicker of ghostly light darting across the ceiling.

"Stay close," I whispered, raising my wand, ready to cast *Recedo* if any spirits got too close. A few ghosts flitted above us, but so far, they hadn't noticed us.

"Let me lead," Sebastian stepped forward.

"You're not immortal," I reminded him, grabbing his arm.

"Here, the last thing you want to be is immortal." He nodded curtly, his eyes serious. Reluctantly, I nodded back at him, letting him take point.

"Keep your eyes peeled," I instructed the team as we moved deeper into the underground city.

"What's that?" Annabelle pointed toward a movement in the shadows ahead.

I narrowed my eyes to look, but before I could make out what I was looking at, a crowd of vampires emerged from the darkness. Their eyes glowed eerily, possessed, and their movements were unnaturally synchronized. Among them, I recognized Ian and Antoine, the former a vampire orphan who had been part of the Underground, and the latter the head of my security team. They looked at me with empty, possessed eyes, no trace of the vampires I knew.

"Mercy Brown," a voice called out, drawing my attention. A vampire stepped forward, one I'd never seen before, his eyes glowing brighter than the rest. "What a surprise. The emperor will be pleased to hear you've given yourself up."

"Given myself up?" I scoffed, brandishing my wand. "I'm here to stop you."

"Brave words," the leader sneered. "But futile. The Emperor's power cannot be contested."

"Guess we'll see about that." I raised my wand, ready to cast whatever spell I needed if the bastard made a move.

"Mercy," Sebastian turned to me, his voice hushed but urgent. "This is too risky. If a ghost gets you, we're all screwed. Let Pauli teleport you out of here."

"Not a chance," I snapped back, eyes locked on the leader. "I'm not running. I'm fighting."

"Are you sure I can't bring out Beli right now?" Annabelle asked.

I glanced at her, seeing the worry etched in her features. She had a point; the situation was rapidly spiraling into chaos.

"Not yet," I sighed. "If it comes to that, do what you have to do."

The ghosts inside the vampires that gathered around their leader started laughing, a chilling, synchronized chorus that echoed off the ancient stone walls. More vampires emerged from the shadows, their numbers swelling until we were surrounded. I recognized most of them—but only a few of them belonged to the Underground. The rest of my team, I assumed, was with Mel accompanying their emperor on whatever errand he was running.

An awkward silence settled into the tension separating my team from the vampires. I knew what that meant. It was the calm before the storm. Each side waiting for the other to make the first move and respond in kind. One thing was clear, though. We were about to throw down.

Sebastian moved first, his gauntlet snapping out a wooden stake that plunged into the heart of an approaching vampire with precision. A random vampire, he'd been turned a decade ago, but I couldn't remember his name. Never the sort who caused me much trouble before—but the ghosts were in charge, now.

I caught a blur out of my peripheral vision. "Donnie, on your left!"

A sickly green glow caught the opposite side of my sight. I spun around. "Recedo!"

The spirit recoiled. I turned back in time to see Donnie's stake tumbling through the air to meet its target in another vampire's chest.

What was going to happen to the staked vamps? Would the ghosts stay in control? That the stakes dropped them now meant that the ancient spirits hadn't totally integrated with the hosts. If they had, not even a stake would drop them. It was good news. If we dealt with the ghosts, I could bring the staked vamps back later.

"Nice throw, Donnie," Annabelle called out, clearly impressed despite the dire circumstances. For a guy who looked more suited for accounting—or plumbing—than combat, he held his own.

"Thanks," he grunted, already preparing his next throw.

"This is pointless!" Sebastian shouted as he staked another vampire. "It's just a matter of time before we're overwhelmed! We need to find the relics!"

"Keep fighting until we get an opening!" I yelled back, though my mind raced with the reality of our situation. "It's hard to play Indiana Jones and track down old relics when you're under attack!"

"Recedo!" I cast again, barely fending off a particularly aggressive spirit. My focus split between protecting myself and attacking the vampires closing in.

"Mercy, watch out!" Annabelle's warning came just in time. I ducked, narrowly avoiding the swipe of a butterfly knife aimed for my throat. I retaliated with a blast of magic, sending the vampire staggering back.

Just when I thought things couldn't get worse, a ghost lunged at me. I felt its cold, ethereal fingers brush my skin, and a shiver ran down my spine. Just as it was about to possess me, a flash of sickly green light illuminated the room.

"Stand down," Mel commanded with a tenor to her voice that wasn't hers. "The vampire queen is mine."

"Like hell I am," I spat back, glaring at her—or rather, at the ancient emperor occupying her body. "You forget, Emperor Qin Shi Huang, I sired the body you're renting."

"Do you really think your pitiful influence is stronger than my presence in this vessel?" The emperor's voice oozed arrogance, his eyes glowing with malevolent glee.

"Let Mel go!" I demanded. "Or I'll destroy you. One way or another."

"Bold words for someone on the verge of defeat," the emperor sneered. "I'll let this body go—your friend will be free if you surrender yourself to me."

I hesitated. My mind raced through possible outcomes. Could I trick him? Was there a way to save Mel without dooming myself?

"Mercy!" Sebastian's voice cut through my thoughts. "Not happening." He appeared out of nowhere, jamming a stake through the back of Mel's heart with precision that only centuries of practice could hone.

"Sebastian!" I screamed, but it was too late. The stake pierced Mel's heart, and she dropped like a marionette with its strings cut.

For a split second, I hoped the emperor would be vanquished. But the hope was dashed as the ghostly form of Emperor Qin Shi Huang rose from Mel's body, his spectral face twisted in rage.

At least I knew Mel could come back. If I could get Sebastian's stake out of her.

"Foolish mortals," the emperor hissed, his ghostly form now floating freely, untethered by any physical vessel. He drifted toward me, waves of pure hatred flowing off him like a magic I'd never encountered before.

"*Recedo!*"

The spell hit him, but he barely flinched. The power behind his presence was overwhelming, suffocating.

"*Recedo!*" I shouted again

It barely slowed him down.

"Pauli!" Annabelle's voice rang out, urgent and commanding. "Get Mercy out of here! Before that ghost takes her over!"

"On it, bitch!" Pauli's boa constrictor form slithered toward me, ready to wrap around and teleport us away. But just as his magic started to shimmer, the emperor ghost sent a shockwave through the air. The force knocked Pauli back, nullifying his magic in an instant.

"Shit!" I cursed under my breath. "No choice, everyone. We have to run!"

We turned to bolt, but our path was blocked. The leader we had encountered earlier stood there, flanked by a horde of possessed vampires, their eyes glowing with malevolent energy. They were everywhere, cornering us like wolves closing in on prey.

"Sebastian," I snapped, trying to keep the panic from my voice, "Any ideas?"

"Run this way," he said, grabbing my arm and pulling me in a direction deeper into the underground labyrinth. "If we can find the relics and destroy them, we can end this here and now."

"Recedo! Recedo! Recedo!"

I cast the spell behind me each time the emperor ghost got too close. It was like trying to swat away a swarm of bees with a feather—ineffective and exhausting. But what else could I do?

"Left here!" Sebastian directed, and we veered into a narrow passageway. I could only *trust* Sebastian's instincts. But how did he know he wasn't leading us into a dead end?

"Are you sure about this, Sebastian?" I shouted as we barreled down the passage. The walls seemed to close in on us, dank and oppressive.

"Not really," he admitted, "But right now I'm running where the ghosts and vampires aren't!"

"Great," I muttered under my breath. "We're screwed."

"Look!" Donnie's voice cut through the chaos. He pointed ahead, where two statues stood against the side of a building, guarding a set of double doors. They were unmistakably two of the terracotta warriors.

"Inside! Now!" Sebastian barked.

We didn't need to be told twice. We burst through the door, slamming it shut behind us. The room was dimly lit, filled with ancient artifacts and scrolls.

But what caught my eye was the old Chinese man standing in the middle, dressed in robes that screamed antiquity. His long hair and beard gave him an air of timelessness, but there was nothing benevolent about the way he looked at us.

"Well, this just got better and better," I grumbled.

"Shén shèng de guǐ dǎn," he intoned, waving his hand. The door behind us sealed with a resounding thud, trapping us inside.

"Anyone catch that?" I asked, sarcasm lacing my words.

"Something about holy ghosts," Annabelle replied, her eyes wide with alarm. Then she gasped, pointing at the floor. "No! That can't be... it's the veve that can be used to summon and bind Baron Samedi!"

"Of course it is," I muttered. "Why wouldn't it be?"

"Annabelle," Sebastian said, trying to stay calm, "What are we dealing with here?"

"This guy is using voodoo. Of course he is. Because he's using vampires as vessels. He had to tap into the Baron's power to make this all work."

"This must be the immortal wizard," Donnie added. "I think we've just met the one who taught the emperor everything he knows."

"Fang-fucking-tastic." I gripped my wand tighter. "Just what we needed."

The veve on the floor pulsed angrily, casting an eerie red glow that bathed everything in a blood-red light.

"Let's take him down!" Sebastian roared, lunging forward, stakes at the ready. Donnie followed suit, his round frame surprisingly agile as he tried to flank the ancient sorcerer.

With a nasal cackle, the wizard flicked his wrist. A shockwave blasted from his hand, sending Sebastian and Donnie hurtling backward like rag dolls.

"Pauli, can you get us out of here?" I shouted, desperation creeping into my voice.

"Sorry, bitch, my magic's still on strike," Pauli hissed, coiled tightly around Annabelle's shoulders, his serpent eyes flashing with frustration.

"Guess it's up to me." I unleashed a barrage of spells, each one more potent than the last, but the wizard deflected them with ease. My own attacks ricocheted back, forcing us to duck and weave to avoid getting fried by my own damn magic.

"Mercy, this isn't working!" Annabelle yelled, her voice cutting through the chaos. She raised her hand. "Beli!"

The air surrounding her hand shimmered as the dragon-spirit dagger materialized, wreathed in green energy.

"Annabelle, what are you doing?" I screamed.

"Getting us out of here," she snapped, not breaking her stride. "You got a better idea? 'Cause we can't best this guy."

"Look!" Donnie's voice rang out, pointing toward a series of statues lining the walls. Their stone-carved eyes pulsed with an energy that matched the ghosts outside, and those possessing my friends. "The statues... they have to be the key. We need to destroy them!"

Sebastian hurled his stake at one of the statues, Donnie following his lead with surprising precision. I fired off a concentrated burst of magic, aiming for the same target. The projectiles struck true, but the statues remained unscathed, as if mocking our feeble attempts.

"Shit," I cursed under my breath, feeling the room grow colder as the wizard conjured a swirling tempest. Wind howled, whipping dust and debris into a frenzy, making it nearly impossible to see or breathe.

"Annabelle!" I yelled over the cacophony. "I don't know about you, but I'm not inclined to stick around to see what that spell will do to us."

"Agreed!" she shouted back. With a swift, practiced motion, she cut through the air with Beli, opening a shimmering portal in the middle of the chaos.

"Everyone, through the portal!" I commanded, grabbing Pauli and pulling him along. One by one, we dove through, leaving behind the malevolent laughter of the wizard and the pulsating veve that threatened to do... well... nothing good.

My feet crashed onto green grass, an otherworldly sun blazing overhead. It didn't burn—because this wasn't *earth's* sun.

"We're in Guinee," Annabelle announced and glanced toward the sky. "And that's Beli's true form. He'll take us back wherever we want to go when we're ready. But we need to sort out what we're dealing with before making another move."

I sighed. Guinee. That's what the vodouisants called it. To druids, like Muggs, it was Annwn. To others it was the Garden of Eden. I'd always called it *the otherworld.*

Bottom line. We'd skipped dimensions. Without Beli, we'd have no way home. But at least now we had a chance to regroup.

"Any bright ideas, anyone?" I asked.

Annabelle sighed. "We pay Baron Samedi a visit."

I snorted. "I thought the wizard was using the Baron. Had him bound somehow."

Annabelle smirked. "You forget, Mercy. When you skip realms, you also skip through time. Where we are now isn't in sync with when the Baron is bound by the Chinese wizard. We *can* find the Baron here, somewhere, and maybe he can tell us how he's being used to force the Emperor and his army into vampire hosts."

Donnie was looking all around, his jaw agape. Sebastian, meanwhile, was seemingly unfazed by our paradisiacal surroundings. "Won't that depend on whether we're here before or after the Baron's experience being manipulated by the wizard?" Sebastian asked.

"Not necessarily," Annabelle explained. "The Loa, what you might think of as demigods or angels, depending on your belief system, aren't temporal beings. They exist in time—but in every time. They also exist outside of any *particular* time."

I chuckled. "No wonder your relationship with Ogoun didn't work out."

Annabelle winced. "Yeah, that was certainly a part of it. I mean, he could shack up with anyone at any time and always tell me that it was his 'old self' that did it, and why should I care, anyway, because his present self was always only with me. At that given moment, only."

"Sounds like a semi-divine load of bullcrap," Sebastian accurately remarked. "But whatever the case, if this Baron has the answers we need, I say we go find him."

I looked all around. "Any guesses where we might find him now? Considering he could be anywhere, and nowhere, all at once?"

"Well," Annabelle thrust her fists on her hips. "We won't find him hiding under a rock somewhere. Thankfully, we have one of his own with us. There's a connection between you and the Baron since he created your kind. Beli can use that to help us track him down."

I bit my lip. "Great. A meeting with Baron Samedi. And I'm the secret code word to get in."

Annabelle nodded. "More or less."

Donnie was still looking around, awestruck. "This is the Garden of Eden?" You'd think he hadn't been listening to anything we'd been talking about. I just nodded at him curtly. "Holy shit! Oops. I mean, poop! Is holy poop a thing? You can't say shit here, can you? You'll get the boot."

I chuckled. "I don't think that's how it works. Just better not eat from the wrong tree."

Chapter 11

THE AIR IN THE Otherworld was thick with an energy that made my skin tingle. Not in a bad way. It wasn't electric, but magical. More like Biofreeze than a finger in the light socket. Pleasant and soothing. As a witch, I was accustomed to such things. As a vampire, even more so. Anything a mortal might feel—especially one with an inclination toward spell craft—was amplified in my senses.

The looks on Sebastian's and Donnie's faces though suggested they felt it, too. And to them, this was a fresh experience. Donnie was almost giddy about it—like a child tasting ice cream for the first time. Sebastian, as was his nature, was more cautious. Optimistic and open-minded, but careful at the same time.

There was no sun here. Nothing celestial shining down on us from outer space. Instead, the entire sky was aglow, like this place was its own light source. I relished in the warmth that washed over my skin. As a vampire, it had been a while since I'd enjoyed anything that resembled such a pleasurable sensation.

Annabelle stood at the center of a clearing, her eyes closed, her arms outstretched. I resisted the urge to roll my eyes. Like, really? Were all the theatrics really necessary?

"Beli," she whispered. Whenever she summoned the dagger on earth, she shouted his name. This time, though, her invocation was more like a prayer.

A roar in the skies above signaled the dragon's arrival. Where had he come from? A portal of some kind? I didn't know. All I understood was that the majestic beast, its scales both golden and green, encircled us as it spiraled toward the ground.

If I didn't know better, I'd think he was a predator descending upon his prey. If it was Oblivion, maybe. But this was Beli. He was good. An agent of creation, not a monster of the void.

"Welcome, Beli," Annabelle said as the dragon landed on the ground without so much as a thump. The beast was large *and* graceful. Like a sumo wrestler with years of training in the ballet.

"Annabelle," Beli's voice rumbled through the clearing, deep and resonant, vibrating in our bones. "You have summoned me in full form. What do you seek?"

"Guidance and transport," Annabelle responded, her voice confident and direct. Wasn't the first time she'd talked to the dragon like this. "We need to find Baron Samedi."

"Climb aboard, everyone," Annabelle instructed, gesturing for us to mount the dragon's back. "Mercy, you ride up front. Place your hands on Beli's head so he can sense your connection to Baron Samedi."

"Basically using me like a GPS?" I tilted my head.

"Precisely," Beli responded, his voice rumbling through the air with an amused tone.

"Wait, did the dragon just talk?" Sebastian muttered, eyes wide as saucers.

Donnie looked equally flabbergasted, his mouth hanging open. "And how does he know what a GPS is?"

"Yes, humans, I do speak," Beli said, his voice laced with a hint of amusement. "Why would you be so arrogant as to think speech originates with your kind? Was it not the Divine who articulated everything into Being?"

"Touché, dragon," I said, trying to stifle a laugh. I had no intention of getting into a metaphysical debate with a creature so ancient. So, I climbed up, settling myself at the front of the dragon's broad neck.

"I still don't know how he knows what a GPS is!" Donnie wasn't letting this go. "He's a dragon from the Garden of Freaking Eden! There are no global positioning satellites here!"

Annabelle sighed. "He and I are connected through the union of Isabelle and myself. He knows what I know. Sort of like he's inside me."

Donnie's eyes widened. "*Inside* of you? How does *that* work?"

"Not like that, dumbass."

I snickered. Donnie really didn't have a clue. Annabelle, as annoying as she could be, was a beautiful and powerful woman. Donnie was… Donnie. He was barely out of t-ball and he was trying out for the major leagues. He clearly didn't know what he was doing.

Still, I had to respect the guy for trying. Even if his comments were doing *nothing* to help his case. Not with a girl like Annabelle. You couldn't flirt your way into her heart. A pick-up-line or twenty wouldn't do. You had to earn her respect—and in my experience, her respect was about as easy to get as Tickle Me Elmo circa Christmastime 1996.

Sebastian and Donnie were next, scrambling up behind me. Annabelle, with Pauli still in snake form around her neck, brought up the rear, just behind Donnie. The dragon's scales felt cool under my hands, almost soothing. I tucked my hands under two of his scales, just for extra grip. I could fall a thousand feet from the sky and survive—if not because I was a vampire, because of where we were. We were in the closest place to heaven that I'd ever reach, but I still suspected that kind of fall would hurt like hell.

"Hey babe... wanna grab onto my love handles?" Donnie's voice dripped with his usual brand of misplaced confidence as he leaned over his shoulder. The comment was obviously for Annabelle.

I looked back, expecting to see Donnie take a slap to the back of his head.

What actually happened was far more entertaining.

Before Annabelle could respond, Pauli slithered down between them in his snake form and shifted back into his human guise. In the blink of an eye, there he was—totally naked, because of course he was. He nibbled on Donnie's ear and purred, "Hey babe back atcha."

The look of horror on Donnie's face was the *definition* of what people used to call a Kodak Moment. He shrieked like a banshee. I imagined something *large* and *in charge* was poking him in the small of his back.

"Dammit, Pauli!" Donnie shrieked.

"What's the matter, sugar? Snake got your tongue?" Pauli blew into Donnie's ear.

Donnie might have jumped off the dragon then and there, but Beli didn't give him a chance. Without warning, he spread his wings wide and launched us into the sky with the force of a hurricane.

The wind whipped past me, tugging at my hair and dress as we soared higher and higher. Below, the Otherworld unfolded in all its surreal glory. We flew over vast expanses of shimmering forests, the boundaries between the Seelie and Unseelie realms visible even from this height. Trees and towering shrooms glowed with an ethereal light, their foliage and crowns like shifting colors in a kaleidoscope. I'd been there more than once—got there through the convergence in the forest near Exeter. It was even more wondrous from the perspective of our dragon's-eye view.

I wondered idly about the timeline here. Was Minerva still reigning over the Unseelie Realm, or had Adam already taken her throne? It was impossible not to think of Ramon, Adam, and Clarissa as we passed by places I recognized from our previous journeys. I missed them all fiercely. Ramon and I had a complex history, of course. But Clarissa was one of my progenies. I was grateful she'd been spared the most recent fiasco. At least she was safe from the Emperor and his ghoulish fiends.

As we ascended further, Beli banked sharply to the right, revealing what looked like an entire kingdom spread out below us. The architecture was strikingly medieval—towers and turrets gleamed in the ambient light, ramparts sprawled across the landscape like the bones of some ancient leviathan. It reminded me of Camelot, the fabled realm of Arthurian legend. At least, what I *assumed* Camelot must've been like.

Beli glided over the kingdom. High enough I couldn't tell if there were guards or knights watching us from below. I couldn't help but wonder what kind of lives people led down there. Did they face the same struggles as we did?

Or was this a place where pain and suffering were mere myths? Were there monsters lurking in the shadows, or was every day a slice of paradise?

The dragon veered sharply again, and the Camelot-like kingdom—or whatever it was—disappeared behind us. The scenery below morphed into something far more somber. Miles upon miles of headstones stretched beneath us, their rigid forms casting long shadows that seemed to reach up like grasping hands. The air grew noticeably colder, and the ever-present light from the firmament above became dim, obscured by thick, roiling clouds.

Baron Samedi's domain. It had to be. What else would the Lord of the Ghede, the Loa of Death, call home than an expansive cemetery? It made *grim* sense.

The dragon descended slowly, almost reverently, before finally landing in the heart of the graveyard. The ground was soft and cold beneath us as we dismounted.

"Where is he?" I asked, scanning the horizon populated by a never ending ocean of tombstones. "Is this where we were supposed to find Baron Samedi?"

Annabelle chuckled softly beside me. "Be patient, Mercy. The Baron likes to make a dramatic entrance."

"Of course he does," I muttered, crossing my arms. "Why wouldn't he?"

The silence that followed was thick, palpable, and awkward. Then, out of nowhere, it was like a giant vacuum sucked whatever warmth was in the air straight out. I was cold-blooded, but this was chilly, even for me.

A low, throaty laugh echoed through the graveyard, and I turned to see him.

Baron Samedi stood before us, emerging from the shadows like a wraith. His face was skeletal, skin stretched tight over bones, making him look more corpse than man. He wore an old-school tuxedo, complete with a top hat that seemed almost comically formal. Yet, nothing about him seemed out of place here.

"Mercy, my child," he purred, his voice like silk dragged over gravel. "I've been expecting you. I knew you'd come one day, eventually, since I've also seen you come now, from the future. Yes, you were bound to seek my help before the end."

I frowned, trying to parse through his cryptic words. "What do you mean, 'the end'?"

The Baron smiled—a chilling, knowing grin that made my blood run cold.

But before I could demand further clarification, Baron Samedi waved his bony hand through the air.

In an instant, the graveyard melted away, replaced by the interior of a house that seemed to have been plucked straight from a fever dream or a horror movie set. Skulls dangled from the ceiling on thin chains, their hollow eyes tracking our every movement. Shrunken heads adorned pedestals, their grotesque features frozen in silent screams.

"Welcome to my humble abode," the Baron chuckled. "Quaint, don't you think? I'm not much for *elaborate* styles."

"Quaint is one word for it," I breathed out. "Not really my cup of tea, though."

The Baron playfully swatted my shoulder. "Oh, you should see Papa Legba's old place! I mean, I try to keep things reserved, subtle, you know. A hint of flourish, a touch of the macabre here and there. But he has entire corpses stretched out for curtains like bear rugs. Faces still attached, of course. Quite delightful, if you're into the finer things."

No one else spoke a word. The legends about Baron Samedi were mostly cautionary tales. Say the wrong thing, speak out of turn, and he might take it as though you were offering a bargain, a deal in exchange for your soul. He pulled out a cigarette, lighting it with a snap of his bony fingers. The sharp scent of tobacco mingled with the musty odor of decay.

He retrieved a flask from his coat and set it on the table. That's how you sealed a bargain with the baron. Take a drink, and your soul was as good as his. Of course, I was the only one of the bunch without a soul to lose. I was a vampire, after all. He already had me. Why, then, had he retrieved the flask? Certainly he didn't expect me to bargain with the souls of my friends.

"Please, take a seat," Baron Samedi instructed, gesturing to a collection of mismatched chairs that looked as though they'd been assembled from desiccated body parts. "There's much to discuss."

"Sure," I muttered as I pulled out a chair and sat down across from him. No one else followed suit. They remained standing. Even Annabelle.

"Come now, everyone. I won't bite. You're my guests. Take a seat, I insist. And open those mouths of yours and speak! You've nothing to fear from me. Not today, anyway."

"Charming place you've got." Sebastian's sarcasm was evident to me—probably not to the Baron. He seemed to agree with the sentiment by tipping his hat at the hunter.

"Thank you, young man," the Baron replied, taking a long drag from his cigar. "It's not often I receive visitors. You'll pardon the... mess. Mrs. Samedi wasn't expecting guests."

I snorted. "You're married?"

"To Maman Brigitte, of course! She'll answer to Mrs. Samedi in a push, but you know how it is. These modern day demigoddesses. Not keen on taking their man's name. To each her own, I suppose."

I sighed. "If you were expecting us, you know why we're here."

"Indeed," the Baron began, leaning forward with an unnerving intensity. "We have much to discuss. The Terracotta Shards, the blood moon, the fate of your world—and your kind."

"Cut to the chase," I snapped, my patience wearing thin. "How did that wizard use you? Somehow he manipulated you so that he could access vampire bodies; put his Terracotta Warrior spirits into us."

"Yes, the wizard." Baron Samedi leaned back, a hint of both red and green flickering in right and left eyes, respectively. A sign that his better or worse natured version of himself could come out at any moment. "Anqi Sheng has naturally been a thorn in my side for thousands of years."

"Naturally?" Annabelle asked. "What does that mean?"

"I am the Loa of Death!" The Baron slammed his fist on the table. The question struck a nerve, clearly. "And that *wizard* found a loop-hole. He escaped me."

"You're pissed that he's immortal?" I asked. "What about us, vampires? You gave us such a gift. Why begrudge him for it?"

"That's different!" Baron Samedi insisted. "I have your souls. Sure, I've given a soul or two back from time to time through the years, but it's always been *my* decision. Anqi Sheng *bypassed* my authority. He spat on my very existence. You must understand. Death is a necessary part of *life*. Without it, nothing can remain in balance. For every mortal who escapes death—and there haven't been many—I must pay the price to suffer what they escaped, lest their... endurance... throw the entire mortal world into chaos."

"Into chaos?" I asked. "What kind of chaos exactly?"

"You've met Oblivion." Baron Samedi narrowed his eyes. "*That* kind of chaos."

"How do we stop Anqi Sheng? How do we save the vampires? We clearly want the same thing here."

Baron Samedi pinched his chin. "There is a way, dear child. But first I must tell you a story."

I snorted. "Story time with death? Yaaaay."

"Patience," Baron Samedi said. "The story I must tell will reveal a path forward, one that you may not be willing to take, Mercy Brown. The tale will conclude with an offer."

Annabelle huffed. "It's always a bargain with you. We won't fall for your tricks."

"No tricks," the Baron said, his eyes still fixed on me. "Not this time. And dare I say it, it will pain me gravely if you accept my terms. You're one of my favorites, you know. Still, you come seeking a path forward, and there is a way. If you will hear it."

I licked my lips. "We're here. And dare I say it, but in this place, we have all the time in the world. But you know me well enough to know I don't have the patience for that much time. Get on with the story so I can know what to do."

Chapter 12

THE ROOM WAS A twisted carnival of grotesquery. It made Ripley's Believe It or Not look like a Precious Moments museum. Skulls with missing jaws and hollow eyes served as lamps, their flickering light casting macabre shadows creeping across the walls. Shrunken heads surrounded us on pedestals. No matter where you moved in the room, it felt like they were watching you.

Like the Mona Lisa. But way freakier.

Baron Samedi pushed his hands into a steeple. "What is wrong, little one?"

I shivered. "Sorry. You said you had a story to tell. I'm just a little distracted by your unique... decor."

"It's quite disgusting." Annabelle said it with such a tone that if she'd chosen different words—or if someone didn't know English—one might mistake it for a compliment. "Reflects your personality."

"Merci, chérie," Baron Samedi replied, his grin as wide as the crescent moon and twice as unsettling. He lounged back in his chair, fingers tapping rhythmically on his polished-bone table. "As much as I'd love to give you the tour of my humble abode, I am not oblivious to the tension in the air."

"We know who you are. And I know what you're doing. This room, all this death, it's a reminder of who you are and what power you have." Sebastian crossed his arms. "I can't speak for everyone, but you don't intimidate me. I'm not impressed. But if your story will show us how to exorcize these ghosts from vampires, we're all ears."

Baron Samedi laughed and gestured at a few of his skulls dangling from his ceiling. "Yes, you do still have all your ears. Unlike my friends here. He who has ears to hear, let him hear."

Annabelle huffed. "You seriously are quoting Jesus right now?"

Baron Samedi laughed. "Another who once escaped my grasp! Death couldn't hold that one. But he did so legitimately, according to his nature. He was no mere mortal. The wizard, Anqi Sheng, however. That's another story."

"Then get on with it and tell us the story," Annabelle insisted, her eyes never leaving the Baron. She's dealt with Baron Samedi two or three times—maybe more—in the past. So far as I understood it, the Baron could be either good or evil—an ally or an adversary. It all depended on which aspect of the Baron you were dealing with at the moment. The green and red glow, one in each eye, suggested we were dealing with all of his personas at once.

Was he a friend or foe? Hard to say, but we needed answers, and if this story held them, I was eager to hear it.

"Anqi Sheng was a powerful wizard, well before he cheated me. He dabbled in arts so dark even the shadows trembled," Baron Samedi began, his voice weaving a spell of its own. "He sought immortality above all else. His hunger for it burned brighter than the stars. But even stars must die. Even they bow to me, eventually. Anqi Sheng never did."

"We know what he achieved," Annabelle said. "How did he do it?"

Donnie and Sebastian each nodded, as if echoing Annabelle's question without words.

"Patience, children," the Baron continued. "I'm getting there. While you know me as Baron Samedi, I'm known by many names to many people."

I nodded. "Right. The Grim Reaper. The Angel of Death."

"To the Egyptians, I was Anubis. The Greeks called me Hades. To the Romans, I was Pluto. I've been called Yama, Mictlantecuhtli, Shinigami, and even a stroke of bad luck, or natural selection. To the atheists out there. But to Anqi Sheng and his people, I was always Yan Wang."

I glanced around the room. "Let me guess, your style has always been this... eclectic."

"Oh, these are just a few of my favorite pieces. I have them on a rotation. I have a collection of fabulous death masks from the Huns that I intend to put on display next month, if you'd care to pay me another visit then."

"We'll pass." I said. "Please continue with the story."

"There is much I could say about Anqi Sheng's exploits. I never took him all that seriously. Many had sought to escape me before, none had ever succeeded. That was my error. I underestimated the wizard's skill and resolve. I thought nothing of it when Anqi Sheng reached the precipice of death, his magic spent. Another mortal dying after wasting his life trying to extend an existence his obsession consumed."

"I'm guessing that's not what happened."

The Baron shook his head. "It's ironic, isn't it? So many waste away their years trying to escape death, so terrified of me they fail to live! Perhaps they seek a fountain of youth, an elixir of immortality, or devote years to a health regimen. Perhaps they fiddle with their genetics and telomeres. Others attempt to create cyborgs, or databases to house their consciousness postmortem. Whether through religion or science, the pursuit of immortality most often comes at the cost of the precious few years of happiness we're given."

"We don't need lessons on serenity and happiness," I said. "I'm guessing Anqi Sheng's magic wasn't spent in the end. He found a way."

The Baron nodded. "He knew then he must face judgment—my judgment. To him, of course, I was always Yan Wang, the King of Diyu. He knew that after years of attempts failed, the only way to defeat death was to deceive him. To deceive me."

I cocked an eyebrow. "You're known for your bargains and crossroads trickery. You're saying a mortal got the best of you"

"How do you suppose I got so good at such deceptions?" Baron Samedi asked. "I was once deceived and thereafter determined never to allow a mortal to best me in a bargain again."

"Hence the birth of the crossroads devil," Sebastian shook his head. "Interesting history to hear directly from death's mouth."

"It took some time to perfect my skill, I admit." Baron Samedi folded his hands together on the table. "I read everything I could on the subject. Rich Death, Poor Death. That's a good one. How to Win Souls and Influence Suckers. Then, of course, who could forget The Art of the Deal."

"We get it," Annabelle said. "You became a master manipulator."

"All because of Anqi Sheng," the Baron continued. "Up until that point, after all, no one had tricked me out of death. Anqi Sheng devised a cunning trick, you see. As he lay on his deathbed, he split his soul in two. One half—the weak, mortal part—he allowed to pass on. The other, the stronger half, he bound into a jade pendant."

"Like a horcrux!" Donnie blurted out. "This guy really is like Voldemort! Sorry, he who must not be named. Not supposed to say it out loud."

I rolled my eyes. "What did he do with the pendant?"

"The wizard had an accomplice. A cunning crane, Yokai, took the pendant and hid it in the deepest part of the Jade Sea," the Baron continued, his hollow eyes staring through us as if he was looking into history—which, perhaps, he was. Considering that he existed outside of time. Hell, he was probably experiencing this story at the same time he was telling it. Confused? Yeah, me too. It's a real mind-fuck when you're engaging timeless demigods. "When Anqi Sheng's spectral form arrived in Diyu, he appeared to me frail. He looked a sorry sight, and I pitied him. He feared in such a state he might reincarnate as a gnat, perhaps a worm. As so many do, he begged for another chance. And as I was sometimes apt to do, I was inclined to grant his request. Provided, of course, he agreed to a bargain."

I rolled my eyes. "The wizard earned your pity?"

"Never again!" the Baron's voice boomed.

"You can see the future, right? I mean, you're timeless. How the hell did he get the better of you?"

Baron Samedi took a deep breath, quelling the storm that the recollection of these events churned in his deathly spirit. "It's not as you think. Any event I experience I do so apart from its consequences—but every action I take reveals to my mind in what you'd call the future the inevitable result of my choice."

"Talk about a mind fuck." I shook my head.

"Not my particular pleasure, but to each her own."

The Baron clearly didn't understand the idiom. The notion of taking a "mind fuck" literally was disturbing, to say the least. Yeah, the Baron said it wasn't his cup of tea. But seeing all the shrunken heads and mangled skulls surrounding us in his room, I had to wonder what he did with them when he was all by himself.

"What were the terms of his bargain?" Annabelle asked. I was grateful she spoke up. It got me past the unfortunate... image... that had manifested in my imagination. Seriously. Are normal people as deranged in their own heads as I am? Probably. But no one else writes about it in their autobiography. Like the one you're reading right now.

"We agreed he might return to earth, broken as he was, and seek to make himself whole again. Should he succeed, I'd grant him a full mortal life full of blessing, and a promise to return to life when he reincarnated into a nobleman's family. But if he failed, which I was sure he would, he'd never return in any form to the world. He'd remain my servant in Diyu forever."

I pinched my chin. "Let me guess, he didn't come back with a new outlook on life. He didn't become whole again by virtue and charity."

"Correct," Baron Samedi said, his tone darkening. "But that's not all. This is how he deceived me. He said a mortal life of blessing, a promise to be reborn in a nobleman's body, was not sufficient. Should he make himself whole again—something I'd never seen a soul in his condition accomplish—he could have a share in my authority, he could bestow the gift of life and death to those whom he chose so long as he might live. And he might also hold the key to his own mortality as a reward."

"You agreed to that?" Annabelle shook her head. "What were you thinking?"

"I was thinking he'd never do it. Again, I'd never seen one with a soul so pitiful as his, recover. I was certain he'd be mine. I'd promised him virtual immortality, I supposed, but he was on the brink of death. I didn't expect in his condition he'd endure another week, much less multiple millennia!"

"Oops." I shrugged.

"I did not agree to the full terms of his proposal," Baron Samedi continued. "I told him that should he succeed, and wished to exercise his authority over others, he could do so only under the condition that he not violate the soul of a willful other. He could grant nothing to anyone whose soul did not consent."

"And vampires don't have souls." I shook my head. "Which is why he's using us. Another loophole in your poorly negotiated bargain."

The Baron shook his head. "The Art of the Deal wasn't as great as its author made it out to be. Shame on me."

I smirked. "So the damned wizard got the best of you, eh?"

"Anqi left the gates of Diyo with the bargain he'd planned to secure all along. He exploited my pity and my arrogance. We'd sealed the bargain with a drink."

"Let me guess," I added. "He came back to life. The Yokai retrieved the pendant, and with a foul ritual, the broken-half of the vile wizard transferred the magical half of his soul back into his body. And since he'd restored himself, he held the key to his own mortality, per the terms of the bargain."

"And the ability to grant my power over other vessels—provided those vessels were absent of souls that could consent to his wishes."

"Typical," I sighed. "Never trust a wizard. It's bad mojo. But I still have questions."

The Baron grinned. "Of course you do."

"Why wait until now? Anqi could have used many vampires through the centuries. He could have brought back the emperor's army at any time."

"I did not tell you the precise wording of our deal," the Baron said. "I granted him my authority over death, but did not promise to teach him how to wield my power. He's had access to my authority for thousands of years. I knew he'd never have the power necessary because the power to wield my authority is mine alone."

"You didn't expect he'd study a little voodoo," Annabelle added. "He learned how to bind you. How to control you."

"He'd tried before," Baron Samedi said. "Many times, in fact, but no other tradition had ever managed to create a ritual that could manipulate me that way."

"It's forbidden in our circles," Annabelle explained. "Not common practice in voodoo. It's the kind of power wielded by the Bokors."

"But you know how to perform the rite. Someone from your community, Miss Mulledy, shared this information with the wizard." The Baron cleared his throat, fixing his eyes back on me. "I am not bound to him here and now, but I am not bound to time or space. I am at once free but always bound to do his will... albeit within a limited time on earth when he's bound my abilities and commanded my power."

"Alright," I started, my voice a mix of skepticism and desperation. "How do we stop Anqi Sheng? And what's the catch?"

"Ah, chérie," Baron Samedi began, his eyes gleaming in the flickering candlelight. "To overcome the one who deceived me into granting him immortality requires a sacrifice." He let the word hang in the air, savoring the tension like a fine wine. "Only another immortal, granted the gift not by my deception but according to my desire, can make that sacrifice."

"Meaning what exactly?" I pressed, my patience wearing thin. "Someone has to give up their immortality?"

"Precisely," he said with a nod. "One must renounce their eternal life. Only then will they gain the power—if they can wield magic—to counteract Anqi's sorcery and reverse the chaos he's wrought."

"Wait," I said, feeling the cold grip of realization tightening around my heart. "Are you saying... I have to give up my immortality? Become human again?"

"Yes," he confirmed, his tone suddenly grave. "You must become mortal once more."

"So I get to trade in my superhuman strength, my eternal youth, and my badass vampire powers in exchange for... my friends and wrinkles?"

"Indeed," Baron Samedi chuckled, a deep, rumbling sound that seemed to vibrate through the very bones of the room. "But there is no deception here, Mercy. The consequences of refusal are dire. If you do not accept this offer, Anqi Sheng will continue to disrupt the balance, and many more souls will suffer."

"No catch?" I exchanged a look of incredulity with Annabelle. "You expect me to believe that?"

"I make no unreasonable demands," the Baron continued, ignoring our exchange. "This is your choice. I've told you how you might gain the power to defeat Anqi Sheng."

"How you might sacrifice me to get vengeance on the asshole, you mean?"

"It's not my sacrifice to make. It is yours. And in exchange, I offer nothing. But it does give you a chance to save your friends. A chance is all I can promise."

"There's no other way?" I cocked my head.

"This is the only solution I can offer," he said, his eyes boring into mine. "And if you refuse, that is your prerogative. But know that more than just your loved ones will pay the price. The emperor will grow his empire. He will change the world."

"And I hate to say it," Annabelle added. "But it'll only be a matter of time before the emperor possesses you. If you aren't a vampire any more, if the Baron is offering you a human soul, he won't be able to harm you."

"He won't be able to possess me, but that doesn't mean he can't hurt me!" I shouted. "I'll be weak! He'll be able to snap my neck, bleed me out, or kill me with a thousand paper cuts. There's no end to the creativity one might employ when killing a human—because your species is so damn fragile. I'll be mortal, Annabelle!'

"Being mortal isn't so bad," Sebastian added. "It's all I've ever known. And I'm alright with it."

I crossed my arms. "This sucks."

"Actually..." Donnie piped in. "It'll mean no more sucking for you."

An awkward silence filled the air.

"Sorry," Donnie mumbled and turned to Sebastian. "Too soon?"

"Great," I sighed, running a hand through my hair. "Just great."

"Remember." Baron Samedi leaned forward in his chair. "This is about redemption as much as it is about sacrifice. It's about saving the people you care about. Not to mention sparing the rest of the world from the vampiric emperor's dominion."

"Annabelle." I turned to her, hoping she'd discerned whatever fine print might have been hidden in the sub-text of what the Baron proposed. "What do you think happens if I do this and fail? The Baron said I'd get the power that might give me a chance to beat the wizard. As a witch, not a vampire. What if I don't beat the wizard?"

"Good question," she agreed, looking pointedly at the Baron. "What's the fine print, Baron? What happens then?"

"Should you fail," he admitted, "you will serve me in death. You will not suffer in vampire hell, for you will no longer be a vampire. But you will remain my eternal emissary forever."

"Sounds like a euphemism for the Baron's eternal bitch," Pauli interjected. "Honey, there's no love lost between us, but as a hougan myself, the last Loa you want to owe eternal servitude to is this one."

"Pauli!" the Baron shook his head. "I'm hurt! I thought we had something special."

Pauli sighed. "I told you that was a one time deal! You didn't pay me enough for the boyfriend experience."

I shuddered. "Another mental image I'd rather forget. But tell me, Baron. If I fail, and I serve you, what happens to my friends?"

"Either way, your sacrifice will restore the balance between life and death. You will either take Anqi's place, the price he offered me once for the bargain he made in poor faith, or you will destroy him and gain what I'd promised him. A comfortable human life. His deal will be fulfilled and the agreement that he can access my power shall be null and void."

"Fantastic." I crossed my arms. "So it's either eternal servitude or a cozy retirement plan."

"Mercy, you don't have to do this." Annabelle took my hand in hers. As if we were besties or some shit. "We'll find another way if we must."

"Another way…" I echoed, staring at the cigarette the Baron gave me. It contained my soul. All I had to do was smoke it and I'd become human again. "What if there isn't another way? What if this is our only chance to save my friends... and the world?"

"Your choice, chérie," Baron Samedi said, leaning back and taking a long drag from a cigar. "But remember, once you leave this realm and return to your time, you'll have little time to act. Anqi Sheng grows stronger by the day."

"My choice." I rolled my eyes. "But you already know what I'm going to choose. Because you exist in the future as much as the past and present."

Baron Samedi grinned widely. "Perhaps I do. But I choose to hold those cards close to my chest."

"Think of it this way," Annabelle offered gently. "If you become human, you'll have a chance at something you lost a long time ago. A real life."

"Yeah." I laughed bitterly. "A real short one."

"Or maybe a fulfilling one," she countered softly. "You could have children. A family, maybe. Or not. The point is you could do whatever you want. You could take a beach vacation. You could sunbathe and risk nothing at all—except maybe skin cancer. But that's not guaranteed either. And it won't be instantaneous. I digress. Whatever you do, you can finally rest."

"Rest is for the weak," I snapped, though my voice lacked conviction. "I've got people to protect. People who count on me."

"Exactly," Sebastian said firmly. "And they need you strong, whether as a vampire or a mortal witch. What you are doesn't change who you are, Mercy. You'll still be you. You'll always be strong. No one can take that from you."

"Fuck," I muttered under my breath, running a hand through my hair again. Could I really trust the Baron, or was this just another elaborate trick? Was becoming mortal worth the risk, worth the chance to defeat Anqi Sheng and save everyone?

"Tick-tock, Mercy," the Baron teased, his rumbling laughter filling the room once more.

"The clock doesn't start until we leave," I growled, tucking my soul-cigarette into my bra. "I'll think about it."

The Baron stood up and gestured to the door. "Either way, I must insist you leave. I have an appointment with the missus!"

"An appointment?" Pauli asked. "You make appointments for that?"

"Doesn't everyone?" Baron Samedi asked. "If you want to take a ride with death, be you my wife or not, you need to get on my schedule."

"Come on," I announced to the team. "Let's get the hell out of here."

"Tsk, tsk!" the Baron raised his flask. "This will only work if we drink on it."

I narrowed my eyes. "Already have the cigarette. Fuck that."

"But that's not all you require! Smoke it and you'll become human, that's true. But you will not have the power you need—my power—to confront the wizard if you do not agree to the deal."

"Same terms as Anqi made," I nodded. "No more, no less."

"Agreed."

The Baron handed me his flask.

"And if I decide not to smoke my soul back into my body?" I asked.

"Then the contract is null and void. You'll owe me nothing. Neither will I have any obligation to you."

I bit the inside of my cheek. "Can I have a vampire turn me back again? Once this is over?"

"Sure," the Baron nodded at me. "But I suspect once you taste mortality again, you'll see things differently."

I shrugged. "Doubt it."

"Keep in mind, should you become a vampire a second time, you will no longer be the progeny of Niccolo the Damned. You will no longer hold a royal bloodline. You will be a youngling. A new vampire. Bound to your maker."

"Yeah, got it." I snatched the flask out of the Baron's bony fingers. Before anyone could stop me, before I could stop myself, I took a swig. It tasted like ass—because a bargain that might make me human again was bound to have a bitter flavor on my palette. But I had a way… a last resort… if it came to that.

But there wasn't any question about it. I knew it when I took the drink. This was the only path ahead. My nights as the bloody queen… were over.

"One more thing," I added. "You said I'd have a new power that I'll need to beat the wizard?"

The Baron nodded as we headed for the door. "Consider it an upgrade to your soul. When you take the puff, you'll feel it. As a witch, you'll know what to do."

Chapter 13

After stepping out of Baron Samedi's cottage, the intoxicating scent of lilies and jasmine hit me like a ton of bricks. But this was paradise. No urge to sneeze followed.

The Otherworld's garden groves sprawled before us—an unnervingly perfect paradise with luscious green grasses that looked too pristine to be real and air so pure it made that oxygen chamber that the King of Pop used to sleep in smell like the skies over Denver.

We walked in silence, each step taking us deeper into this surreal Eden. There wasn't a rush when you were in another world, outside of the timeline that defines our own. No one said a word. They were waiting for me to tell them it was okay. To make a decision. To smoke that damned cigarette.

The irony. Smoking in paradise. That shit wasn't in Genesis at all. Eat from any tree you want. Except that one.

It's naughty. And don't smoke those leaves. They'll kill ya, too!

"I don't want to be a real girl," I muttered as I kicked an innocent blade of grass in front of me.

"Take all the time you need," Annabelle said. "I know this is a big decision. I think you know what has to be done, but no one is going to tell you to do it. If you want to find another way, try to beat the wizard some other way..."

"There is no other way."

"I'm just saying. I understand how hard this is for you. You've been a vampire for... several lifetimes longer than you were human."

I shook my head. "It's not just what I'm giving up. It's what I'll become. Would you want to be something you eat?"

"I can be a dick sometimes," Pauli added. "And I eat..."

"Stop!" Annabelle chuckled as she backhanded Pauli on the shoulder.

I tried not to laugh, but a small chuckle escaped my lips. "What if someone told you, 'Hey, you can save your friends, but you have to become a chicken nugget first?'"

"Humans aren't chicken nuggets," Sebastian said. "And you don't see us like that, either. I know you. You save people's lives. I've seen you risk your life more than once for humanity. I've never once risked a damn thing for a chicken nugget."

I laughed a little. It made sense, I guess. "You're right. Being human isn't that bad. We vampires, though, we don't handle change well. And this is as big as it gets."

"Mercy, I know I keep saying it, but we're not on a clock here. As soon as we go back to the world, we'll have to act fast. We need to make sure we have a plan now before we decide. And you need to be sure you're comfortable with your choice."

"All the time in the world. Tell that to my sanity." My sarcasm aside, she was right. But having time didn't make it easier. I'd already had more *time* in my existence than any human who'd ever lived. Who was I to demand more time now?

"Maybe I should just count my blessings. It's been a good run."

"You heard what he said," Annabelle added. "You can become a vampire again..."

I laughed. "And start over as a youngling? That would be like an alcoholic with thirty years of sobriety getting drunk and having to go back to a meeting to pick up a twenty-four-hour chip. I don't know that I could go back to being just some young, bloodthirsty monster again."

"That might be sort of how it's like," Sebastian said. "But even if a drunk goes out after thirty years, that doesn't mean his time in sobriety didn't count. It's not starting over. It's a new chapter. But you can have a new chapter as a human, too. You can always become a vampire again. You might not get a third chance at *life*."

"Whenever you're ready," Annabelle continued, "I can summon Beli, and he'll take us back to confront the wizard."

"Say I do this." I stopped walking and stared at the pristine horizon ahead. "What's the plan? Because even if I give up... everything... and get the magic I need to beat this damned wizard, we have to make sure we're breaking all the statues or whatever relics these souls are rooted in. If we don't do that, and the ghosts merge with my friends... we'll lose them forever. Even if I manage to beat the damned wizard."

Sebastian nodded, his face a mask of grim determination. "You're right, Mercy. We need a plan. A solid one."

Donnie scratched his head right where his horseshoe hairline met his turtle-waxed dome. "And there's no guarantee those terracotta statues we saw in the wizard's lair account for all the spirits out there. For all anyone knows, that's barely a drop in the bucket. There could be thousands more in that underground Chinatown or hidden somewhere else entirely."

"Thought of that," I muttered, rolling my eyes. "And if I'm a human, I'll be more vulnerable than ever. Even if we destroy the statues in the wizard's lair, and it destroys some ghosts and frees a few of the vampires from their thrall, there might still be dozens in that underground city just waiting to pounce on us. How the hell are we going to get out of there alive?"

"Me, duh," Pauli added. "I can take you straight out of there and back home. Easy peasy, boa constrictor squeezy!"

I chuckled. "Right, of course. I'm not thinking clearly."

"It's understandable," Annabelle added. "Like I said..."

"Yeah, yeah. Take my time. I know. But we still need to figure out a way to be absolutely sure we've found and destroyed all of those... whatever they are..." I trailed off, trying to find the right words.

"Horcruxes," Donnie added, his tone annoyingly smug.

"Ugh, they're not called that! That's from a book, dumbass," I snapped. My rebuke came out harsher than I'd intended. "Sorry. I'm just on edge about all of this. It's nothing personal. But this isn't Harry Potter. They aren't horcruxes. That's not even a freaking word."

"Fine, miss witchy witch." Donnie's smirk was infuriating. "You're the expert on magic and all. What would you call them?"

I paused, tapping my fingers against my thigh in thought. "Soul-containing thingies." As soon as the words left my mouth, I realized how ridiculous it sounded. The others burst into laughter, and despite myself, I couldn't help but crack a grin. For a brief moment, the tension melted away.

"It's settled," Annabelle said, wiping a tear from her eye. "We *must* destroy every last soul-containing thingy out there."

"It doesn't matter how long we take. We don't know enough about the wizard's magic and how the souls are bound to their... thingies... to know how to find them." I pinched my chin. "But if we don't try we'll never end this. Let's get to it."

"Are you sure?" Annabelle asked, her eyes searching mine for any sign of hesitation.

"Absolutely," I said, with more conviction than I felt. "I say you call Beli, Annabelle. Have him take us straight back to the wizard's lair. Let's kick his ass and get this over with."

"Alright then," Annabelle replied. But she didn't summon Beli yet. She knew as much as I did that I had something I had to do first. She looked at me and nodded. A gesture meant to show support. Maybe it would mean more to me *after* my smoke. After I became human again.

I reached into my bra, retrieving the cigarette that Baron Samedi had given me. My soul, neatly rolled and ready for consumption. No surgeon general warnings on this one. But it would have been appropriate. Because eventually, some day, hopefully not in ten minutes... this thing *would* kill me. "Anyone got a light?" I asked, holding up the cigarette.

"Yeah, sure," Donnie said, fishing out a lighter from his pocket. He flicked it open and held the flame to the end of the cigarette. As the tip flared to life, I took a deep drag, filling my lungs with smoke—and my soul.

The transformation hit me like a freight train. My limbs felt like lead, my senses dulled. The world around me blurred and spun. Sebastian's powerful arms caught me before I could hit the ground.

"Whoa, I've got you." His voice was like a tether anchoring me to reality.

"Thanks," I muttered, trying to steady myself. I was weak. So weak.

For a second.

Then a surge of power coursed through me, igniting every nerve ending with raw, unfiltered energy. This was what the Baron had promised. The magic I'd need to kick that wizard's ass back to the land before time.

"How do you feel?" Annabelle asked, her eyes wide with concern and curiosity.

"Powerful," I said, though my voice sounded distant even to my own ears. Then a wave washed over me. Exhaustion. I hadn't felt so... sleepy... since...

Sebastian steadied me again.

"I think she needs a little sleep," Annabelle assessed. Damn, she really knew how this human shit worked. "Don't fight it, Mercy. Get your rest. We'll be here when you're ready."

"Just... think about how we'll find all those soul-containing thingies," I mumbled, fighting to stay conscious. "Can't let that bastard win."

Chapter 14

"Here Comes the Sun" played like a phantom soundtrack, and I couldn't figure out where the music was coming from. The serene guitar strums felt like they were mocking me.

I huffed and muttered to myself. "Of all the Beatles' songs...why this one? How about 'Helter Skelter'?"

As if on cue, the tune morphed into the chipper notes of "Good Day, Sunshine."

Another Beatles number. Not my favorite. "Have anything from the White Album?"

The song kept playing. Whatever DJ was hiding in the clouds had apparently declined my request.

"Whoever's out there playing this shit, I get it. You have a sense of humor. Hil-arious."

That time they heard me. The soundtrack changed the song again. That damn Johnny Nash song. You know the one. About how it's going to be a bright, sunshiny day.

I was picking up on the theme. It wasn't a Beatles theme... it was the goddamn sun!

I was walking in broad daylight, and my skin wasn't sizzling off my bones. "That's right... I became human... but why am I here?"

The sand between my toes felt oddly comforting, each grain a small reminder that I was... *alive.*

I stepped into the surf and let the waves wash over my feet. It felt so different—so real. I laughed.

"Well, this is new," I said, lifting my arms and twirling like a ballerina—though without the grace, given I was in sand and didn't have the training. It differed from the Otherworld's light. On this beach, the sun was blazing in the skies above. "I wonder if I can... tan?"

I'd been so pasty for so long, I was probably in for a sunburn. Nothing like the burn I'd suffer as a vampire, though.

"A base tan," I pinched my chin. "That's what they call it, I think. A few minutes in the sun today. A few more tomorrow. Build it up over time."

I shrugged. Whatever. I'd figure that out later. I started running around, letting the sun drench me in its golden warmth. It was intoxicating. Euphoric. I hadn't realized how much I'd missed this simple pleasure. Hell, I grew up in Exeter, Rhode Island. I'd never been to a beach even as a human...this was my first time *enjoying* a beach in...forever!

My laughter echoed across the empty beach, mingling with the sound of crashing waves.

"Having fun, are we?" A familiar voice, smooth as aged whiskey, cut through my euphoria.

I stopped dead in my tracks, spun on my heel, and there he was...

Nico.

My former sire. He'd got his soul back from the Baron, too. Smoked his soul into his flesh. Then...well...

Let's just say he died. That's what he wanted. After thousands of years, he'd grown weary of his existence. I didn't understand it at the time. Still didn't completely. How could anyone understand what it was like—vampire or not—to exist for thousands of years?

That damn wizard did... but he didn't share Nico's former death wish. If he did, things would be a lot easier.

I looked Nico over. Exactly how I remembered him. Tall, dark, and wise.

He stood there staring at me, arms crossed, an amused smirk playing on his lips.

"Wait," I said, squinting at him. "This is a dream, isn't it?"

"Indeed, it is."

"So it's not real?"

"Who's saying dreams aren't real? What if this is the real world, and the other place is the dream?"

"Stop fucking with me, Nico."

"See, vampire or not, you're still the same Mercy." He chuckled, his laughter rich. I'd almost forgotten how…comforting…his laugh could be. It was like everything was the way it was supposed to be. It made me feel safe.

"But you're really you…"

"Dream or not, it's me."

"Okay. But what are you doing here?"

"Surely you've heard." His tone was almost playful. "I'm among the Loa now. I was divinised in death."

I sighed. "I hear a lot of things. Hailey said something about that."

"Then none of this should come as a surprise."

I scratched my head. I fell asleep in the Otherworld. Just after I'd inhaled my soul on the cherry of Pall Mall. Were human dreams always so vivid? I couldn't recall. It had been so long.

"Fine, this is a dream. But you can show up in my dreams. What's the news? Am I mysteriously with a child destined to save the world?"

"The virgin Mercy?" Nico laughed. "Please. You may have found favor with the Divine…but this isn't that."

"Then why are you haunting my beach party?" I crossed my arms over my chest.

"Let's just say that Baron Samedi owed me one." Nico stared at me with a kind of fatherly affection. His eyes. That was one thing that was different. They were so *dark* now. As a vampire, they had always been blood red…like mine…I mean, like mine used to be. I hadn't had a chance to catch my reflection yet.

"He owed you one?" I tilted my head. "What did you do for him? No one wants to be in the Baron's debt."

Nico shrugged. "It doesn't matter. Suffice it to say, the power he mentioned you'd get to help beat the wizard? It's me, Mercy."

I tilted my head, narrowing my eyes at him. "What do you mean, it's you? You're a spell or something?"

"Not quite." Nico shook his head slowly. "Think of it more like..an aspect. Annabelle has the aspect of Ogoun, the Loa of War. It's why she's such a great fighter. Pauli has the aspect of Aida-Wedo, the Loa of snakes and rainbows. That's how he teleports and shapeshifts."

"I know how that works." I wasn't into voodoo magic, but I'd been in New Orleans long enough to understand the basic mechanics. "Okay, so…what power do you have?"

"You might consider me the Loa of Balance," he said.

"Balance?" I raised an eyebrow. "What does that even mean?"

"It means I put things back where they belong," Nico explained, his tone growing more serious. "When people make a mess of things, whether with magic, technology, or whatever, I clean it up."

I snorted. "So you're the janitor of the gods?"

Nico laughed again, shaking his head. "We aren't really gods, Mercy. Closer to what you'd call angels. But call us what you will. I have a job to do, and that's that. It's a bit more glamorous than taking out the trash and cleaning bathrooms."

"Sure," I said, rolling my eyes. "How will this help me beat Anqi Sheng? We're going to do his dishes, mop his floor, and clean his shitter?"

"You don't understand," Nico replied without hesitation. "Anqi Sheng violated the natural order. He needs a little cleaning up."

"Balance...right. You don't just clean up messes. You fix what's broken. You're more like the Tim Allen of the gods."

"Tim Allen is an actor. You're really dating yourself with that reference. Home Improvement. Really, Mercy?"

I shrugged. "It's not that old. Relatively speaking. It's not like I was invoking the memory of Charlie Chaplain."

"Fair enough," Nico said, smirking. "But yeah, think of me as the cosmic handyman. And Anqi Sheng...well, he's a pretty big repair job."

"Great," I muttered, kicking at the sand. "So, you're saying when I face this ancient wizard who's been cheating death for millennia, you'll pop in and fix everything?"

"Not everything," Nico corrected, his tone softening. "But I'll be there to help. I've always been with you, Mercy. Always watching your back, even if you didn't know it."

"Yeah?" I looked up at him, a mixture of skepticism and hope in my eyes. "Then why do I feel so damn alone sometimes?"

"You've never been alone," he said simply. "Do you realize how many people...vampires, rather...look up to you? You give them hope."

I took a deep breath. Something I actually *had* to do at regular intervals as a human now. At least I would when I woke up. "Well, those days are over."

"You think your vampirism made you a hero, Mercy?"

I shrugged. "My magic helped a little. But yeah. I couldn't have kicked all the asses I kicked through the years if I wasn't a vampire. But now...as a human...I'll be so damn—"

"Vulnerable?" Nico smiled at me—no fangs now, either. That was another difference I didn't think I'd ever get used to. Then again, as I traced my tongue over my teeth, I realized mine were gone as well.

I nodded. "Right. That."

"Vulnerability sucks, I get it. But it's also what makes you strong."

"Sounds like bullshit weak people say to make themselves feel better."

Nico laughed. "Not at all! You've always *had* vulnerabilities, Mercy." Nico gestured out toward the ocean. We watched a moment as a wave crashed ashore and the water creeped up the beach toward our feet. "Are you afraid of sharks?"

I shrugged. "I suppose I should be. Now that I'm human."

"If you're in the ocean, you might have a reason to be. On the beach, though…sharks are pussies."

I laughed. "Right. Not too scary when they're flopping around on shore."

"In the ocean, they're practically invulnerable. They are an apex predator. A dolphin might fend one off, but there's not much out there that can kill a shark. Put it up on the beach, though, and it's a different story. The shark is vulnerable. To the elements, not just to those who might do it harm."

"Right. So as a vampire, I'm deadly at night. Weak as shit during the day. I get the metaphor."

"The point is that you've always been vulnerable, Mercy. You learn to work around your weaknesses to minimize them as much as possible. But not being able to go out during the day *does* limit us—well, it limits what we used to be."

"Well, as a human, you can kill me during the day, you can kill me at night."

"But you *can* fight in the light now. Couldn't do that before. Not without those ridiculous kevlar suits you all use in the Underground."

I tilted my head. "How do you know about all of that?"

Nico laughed. "The Baron sees everything you do. Vampires are his eyes in the world. He's let me look in on you a few times."

"Creeper." I laughed.

"Not like that," Nico winked at me. "I've watched *over* you. That doesn't mean I've been watching you Peeping Tom style."

"I get the point," I said. "Maybe I stand a better chance fighting bad guys at high noon than I did before. Eventually, though, I will die. Every human does. I had a fighting chance at immortality before."

"Even vampires die, eventually." Nico added. "It's the law of averages. How many times do you think you can get lucky saving the world before someone does you in?"

"As many times as it takes."

"And on the scale of *eternity*... eventually someone would eliminate you. It's just how it works. Vulnerability isn't about your weaknesses. It's about how much you allow those weaknesses to hold you back."

"I think I get it. You're saying that I can use this to my advantage. Because I'm fighting ghosts who are suffering from the weaknesses of their vampire bodies."

"Pretty much," Nico replied. "When you face Anqi Sheng, ask for my help, and I'll be there. We'll put things back where they belong. Together."

Together...

"Dude, you belong in one of those Christian Bookstores. So damn sentimental. What happened to the Niccolo the Damned I used to know?"

Nico laughed. "I prefer to be called Niccolo the Blessed. It's more fitting."

"Not nearly as badass, though."

Nico smirked. "Well, we can workshop the moniker. Maybe I can be Niccolo the Slightly Inconvenienced."

I rolled my eyes. "Really living on the edge with that one."

"Niccolo the Fix-it-Guy!"

"Nope. Doesn't work."

"Niccolo the Well-Adjusted. Niccolo the Balanced. None of these work."

"Maybe you should change your name to a symbol. We'll call you the demigod formerly known as Niccolo the Damned."

Nico shook his head. "Ah, I met Prince. Since I'm technically aligned with the Ghede, it was inevitable. After he died. He regretted that move. He strongly advised against turning a multi-million dollar brand into an emoticon."

I shrugged. "Didn't matter, though. The symbol didn't stick because he was always Prince to the rest of us. Purple

Rain was just as amazing no matter what people called him."

"Then call me what you like," Nico said. "But consider the same is true for you. You might not be the bloody queen, the last surviving and favored progeny of the original vampire. But you're still you. And you can sing all the same songs."

I cleared my throat. "See my previous comment. Christian bookstores and Hallmark Cards. You're so warm and fuzzy now!"

"But I'm still the Nico you always knew." My former sire pulled me into a hug. "And you'll always be my Mercy."

"Gag…gag…gag!"

We laughed together about that. Our voices melding into one. Until the scene of the beach, Nico's calming touch, the smell of the sea all faded away.

"I think she's awake," Sebastian's voice said as I shielded my eyes. In a split-second, he was leaning over me. "And she's human. Look at those dark brown eyes."

I snorted. "Screw you."

Sebastian laughed. "Mercy's back, everyone. You ready to go teach this wizard a lesson?"

I hopped up—with more energy than I'd expected. "I think so. How long was I asleep?"

"How long?" Annabelle laughed. "Let's just say it's hard to keep track of time in this place. But you've been down for at least sixteen hours, give or take."

I shook my head. "Haven't slept that well in a century. And the dreams..."

"What kind of dreams?" Pauli asked. "They were about me, weren't they? Hate to break it to you, Mercy, but while I might be the man of your dreams..."

"You aren't," I quickly added. "And I know I'm not your type."

Pauli put his arm around Donnie. "This guy, on the other hand..."

Donnie shrieked and jumped away. I didn't blame him. Pauli was totally naked. "How many times do I have to tell you! I'm straight!"

"Right!" Pauli winked at Donnie. "Straight as a circle."

"It's the truth!!!" Donnie insisted. "I like women. *WOMEN!*"

Pauli shrugged. "I can put on a dress if you'd like. Everything about me is fluid, you know."

Donnie shook his head. "Fluid my ass."

"If that's where you want it!"

I couldn't help but laugh. "I know you're embracing this whole Garden of Eden vibe, with the traditional dress and all—which is nothing at all."

"Fig leaves are in fashion from time to time," Annabelle quipped.

"GET DRESSED, PAULI!" I shouted. "We have an immortal wizard to fight."

Pauli sighed and shook his head. "Fine... if I must."

Annabelle tossed Pauli her backpack. Then she looked up at the sky for a moment. She looked back at me. "Last chance, Mercy. Ready for this?"

I nodded and cracked my neck. Ouch. That felt different now. I retrieved my wand for good measure. "Let's end this."

Chapter 15

BELI'S SCALES SHIMMERED BENEATH us, reflecting an almost ethereal glow as we soared through the sky. The dragon's breath ripped open a portal, swirling with hues of indigo and emerald. We plunged through it, gravity giving way to chaos, until solid ground greeted us harshly. My knees buckled under the impact, but I caught my balance just in time to see familiar surroundings.

"Where the hell is he?" I demanded. The wizard's sanctuary was eerily silent and cold. My new found warm-bloodedness made me a lot more sensitive to temperature. One of a thousand adjustments I'd have to get used to in time.

Sebastian dusted himself off and adjusted his coat. "He can't have gone far. Did the dragon bring us back to when we'd left?"

"Seconds later," Annabelle confirmed, clutching Beli now transformed into a dagger. "He's here somewhere."

"Maybe," I conceded, irritation bubbling beneath my skin. "He's a wizard, remember. And the power he knows... as old as he is... there's no telling what he can do. Teleportation isn't off the table."

"Which means he could be anywhere," Pauli added.

"Shit," I muttered, surveying the room. "Why would he leave us here with all these statues?"

The terracotta warriors loomed around us, their eyes glowing that sickly green that also filled the eyes of my possessed friends. That the light still shone in the statues, though, was a good thing. It meant that the souls of the emperor's warriors hadn't fully integrated with their vampire bodies. My friends could still be saved.

"We still can't destroy them," Sebastian said. "He knows as much. Leaving them here isn't a risk."

"The wizard doesn't know that I can stop him," I said. "Maybe he's out there somewhere looking for us? Maybe he didn't realize that Annabelle's portal took us to the Otherworld."

Donnie shrugged. "As good a theory as any."

I sighed. "I can't even sense Mel's presence anymore. My progenies aren't... *mine* anymore. Didn't think about that when we made this decision.

"Not the end of the world," Sebastian said. "I don't usually have a supernatural tether to the monsters I hunt. And I *always* find them. Eventually."

"Mercy," Annabelle interjected, glancing at me with those penetrating eyes of hers. "Do you know what the spell is that you're supposed to use? If we encounter Anqi? Baron Samedi said you'd *know*."

I nodded sharply. "I know what to do."

I didn't have the words—or the time—to explain how I knew. I didn't tell them about the dream. It didn't matter. Useless information that we could discuss later—if we survived this shitshow. To talk about it now would only waste time. What mattered is if we found that damn wizard, I could take him.

"First, we find Anqi Sheng," I continued. "Once we deal with him, we should be able to destroy the statues." I locked eyes with each member of our ragtag team. "Finding the wizard is the priority, not fighting possessed vampires."

"Right," Annabelle said, twirling Beli in her right hand. "Let's get this bastard."

"Just remember," I added, my tone colder than ice, "Anqi Sheng has outsmarted death itself. Don't underestimate him for a second."

"Follow me," Sebastian said. "This isn't the first dungeon hunt I've been on. Won't be the last."

If I were still a vampire, I might have protested and taken point myself. But I wasn't. I had to keep in mind my newfound vulnerabilities as a human and not rush in headstrong per usual.

I wasn't a shark anymore. Or maybe I was. But I needed to stay in my element. I think that was the point of what Nico told me in my dream.

If I stuck to my strengths now... as a witch... even as a human...

That was the key. Make the enemy fight me in *my* environment, on my playing field. Where I had the advantage.

How many hours until sunrise? I didn't know. But I couldn't guarantee that we had that much time before the ghosts integrated with my friends' bodies. Even so, I didn't want to burn them to death. I didn't want to encounter them at all.

The only way to get the upper-hand in this fight was to *avoid* the possessed vampires and find Anqi Sheng again. Beat him, and we win.

I was his kryptonite now. Even if I was mere *food* to the vampires. Food that could cast spells and would fight like hell—but food, no less.

"Stay close," Sebastian whispered. He led us through the maze-like corridors of the underground Chinatown. The air was thick with the scent of mildew, stone, and something else. Something foul. Probably the accumulation of several decades of body odor, sewage, and whatever else.

I'd overlooked the scent before, as a vampire, when the smell of blood took front and center. Now it was just the common human stink that dominated my olfactory senses.

"He's got to be here somewhere," I muttered, more to myself than anyone else. "If we can just—"

"Shhh," Sebastian hissed, holding up a hand. He crouched low, peering into the shadows ahead. "We're not alone."

"Who is it?" I asked, my heart pounding. That was new.

"Can't tell," Sebastian replied, his words wrapped in tension. "But something's moving."

I narrowed my eyes. Can't see in the dark anymore. Another thing to check off on my list of abilities lost. But I did see the shadow, something or someone lurking between the buildings just ahead.

Then a flash of magic. Had to be the wizard.

I started to take off after the son of a bitch, but suddenly, the ground beneath us trembled. Dust cascaded from the ceiling, and the walls groaned ominously.

"That can't be good," Pauli said, doing his best impression of Captain Obvious.

"The damn wizard!" Annabelle shouted. "He's trying to bury us alive in here!"

"Fan-fucking-tastic," I growled. No more 'fangs' in my trademark expletive. For obvious and disappointing reasons. "Everyone, move! We have to catch that fucker before this place comes down around us!"

The ceiling started to crack, sending chunks of debris raining down. The sound was deafening, a cacophony of destruction that drowned out even our frantic breaths. The once-stable buildings of subterranean Chinatown began to crumble, their foundations giving way to the magically induced quake that the wizard cast over the place.

"Go, go, go!" I shouted, pushing Sebastian forward. "I just have to get a hand on that motherfucker and we can end this!"

"Not if we're buried first!" Sebastian shot back, darting ahead as another chunk of ceiling crashed down behind us.

"Pauli!" Annabelle's voice cut through the chaos. "Get everyone out of here! Take them back to Mercy's underground!"

"On it!" Pauli responded with a wicked grin, his rainbow-colored scales shimmering as he shifted into snake form. He wrapped himself around Donnie first, who was looking more terrified by the second. In a flash of iridescent light, they vanished.

"Annabelle, your turn!" I barked, dodging a falling beam. "You get out of here. I'm going after the wizard!"

"Mercy! You have to come, too! We can rally outside. Come at him again. But you can't survive if this place collapses on you. Not any more!"

"Take her, Pauli!" I insisted.

He didn't question the order. I would not argue with Annabelle about the mission. All I needed was to get a hand on that asshole. His expiration date had long-since come due, and it was time to get rid of him once and for all.

"Sebastian, you're up next!" I shouted, my eyes scanning for any sign of the wizard. But all I could see were collapsing structures and rising dust clouds.

"Be careful, Mercy," Sebastian said before Pauli wrapped around him and whisked him away.

"Don't worry about me," I muttered, more to myself than anyone, because by the time I got my words out I was the only one who remained.

I caught another flash of light in the distance. I didn't know what it was, but it *was* magic. The wizard was still there.

I took off running. Damn, I was slow! If I was still a vampire, I'd have caught up to him in a second. But now…

The floor beneath me buckled, throwing me off balance. I stumbled, barely catching myself before a fissure split open at my feet.

"Time to go, darling." Pauli's voice slithered into my ear, his snake form already coiling around me.

"Wait, not yet—" I started, but then everything blurred into a kaleidoscope of colors as the teleportation spell took hold. The sensation was disorienting, more so now as a human. It was like being spun in a centrifuge that was mounted on a roller coaster. My stomach flipped, and my vision swam.

Nausea. And I hadn't even had a proper human meal yet.

My feet landed hard on the cold stone floor of the Underground. I rubbed my eyes. We were near the elevators, down the hall from the security room. A short jaunt to my throne room.

"We need to get back there!" I insisted. "The wizard is still in whatever's left of Chinatown."

"You really think he's not going to just teleport out of there like we did?" Annabelle asked.

I shook my head. "We don't know what he can do. But we need to start where we last saw him if we're going to catch him in time."

"Not so fast." I spun around to the sound of a familiar voice.

It was Juliet. She was out of her cell. Then Muggs stepped up behind her.

"Shit."

"Pauli!" Annabelle shouted. "Now!"

But then a blast of magic. That damn snot-colored mana I'd seen so much of as of late. It came from another figure approaching us from further down the hall.

"No, no, no," Mel said—rather the ghost who'd apparently re-claimed her as his host. "Bad snake. No magic for you."

I turned away. I couldn't let them see my eyes. If they knew I was mortal...

"What have we here?" Mel purred, her chilly hand touching my cheek. Sebastian came after her, but with a wave of her hand, he crashed into the wall.

"Beli!" Annabelle shouted.

"No, wait!" I screamed. She was going to hit Mel with that dagger. It would stop the emperor, but it would damn Mel, too!

"*Enerva*!" I screamed, aiming my wand. It hit Annabelle, who fell to the ground totally immobile.

Emperor Asshole laughed. "Ah, Mercy. So soft...so sensitive...whatever have you done to yourself?"

I snorted. "Can't take me now, bitch."

The emperor smiled widely. "We'll just have to see about that, won't we?"

The next thing I knew, Mel's fangs were in my neck.

So much for being human.

Chapter 16

THE ROOM SPUN LIKE a carousel from hell, each rotation punctuated by the memory of Mel's bite sinking into my neck. My vision blurred, and the hunger hit me like a freight train—blood. I craved it, needed it. Damn it, I was a vampire again.

Best laid plans gone to shit.

I knew what was coming next. The emperor had plans for me to use me as his "blood queen" to rally the others. Just what I needed in my already chaotic life.

Of course, I wasn't technically the vampire I used to be. I was a youngling. But the emperor clearly didn't understand all of that. I wouldn't have an effective sire bond to use on anyone. Then again, maybe it was my magic he craved.

Suddenly, a wave of sickly energy washed over me, making my skin crawl. I tried to move, but I was pinned down.

Juliet and Muggs—no, the ghosts possessing them—had me trapped. Their eyes were vacant, the color of pea soup. They were puppets on spectral strings.

"Get off me, you bastards!" I snarled, struggling against their grip. But they held firm. They were stronger than me, now.

I glanced over at Mel, slumped lifelessly on my throne, her body limp as a rag doll. My barely beating heart clenched as I saw a noxious fog flow out of her mouth. It was the ghost…the emperor…and he was coming for me. The ghost—no, the emperor—was pouring out of her mouth like a noxious fog.

Shit, I thought. *Here it goes.*

As the last wisp of fog left Mel's lips, it turned its attention to me. The room grew colder, and my breath came out in visible puffs. It was like being dunked into an ice bath, except this ice bath wanted to crawl into my skin and wear me like a suit.

"Not today, Emperor Asshole," I muttered through gritted teeth. But it was too late; he was already inside me. I could feel him like a poison in my veins, cold and relentless.

Mercy, a voice echoed in my mind, steady and familiar. Nico.

I'm still here. Do not be afraid.

You're still here??? I thought right back at him.

Remember what the Baron said, Nico continued. *You had to offer a sacrifice of your immortality. You did that.*

Wait, so I don't have to be human?

That's not what the Baron said, Nico clarified. *Your sacrifice was enough. What was important is that you were willing to give up your immortality for your friends. Now focus!*

Focus

It was easier thought, than done. The emperor's presence grew stronger, pushing at the edges of my consciousness. My vision blurred, and dark spots danced around the corners of my eyes.

"Mercy!" Mel's voice cut through the fog of my mind, sharp and commanding. "As your sire, I command you to resist! Expel that motherfucker to hell!"

Holy crap. Mel is using her sire bond on me now...

Her words were like a lifeline thrown into the stormy sea of my mind. I felt a surge of strength coming from the bond I hadn't even realized we shared. It was weird as hell, but maybe...just maybe, it could work.

Focus, Mercy! Nico's voice echoed again. *We can do this, but it will take all of us!*

I gathered every ounce of willpower I had, focusing on the core of my being. I imagined a barrier between me and the emperor, something impenetrable, something he couldn't cross. It was like trying to hold back a tsunami with a sandcastle, but I had to try.

"Get. Out. Of. My. Head!" I roared, feeling the strain as the emperor fought back, his presence like icy claws digging into my brain. But with Mel's command giving me that extra push, and Nico's steady encouragement, I started to push back.

My wand was strapped to my leg. I grabbed it and jammed it into my jugular. "*Recedo!*"

I couldn't usually cast magic on myself. Most witches can't. But I wasn't aiming it at *me*. I was attacking the emperor *inside* of me.

It was working!

I felt the emperor's grip loosen, just a fraction, but it was enough to give me hope.

Again, Mercy! Nico urged. *You can do this!*

"*Recedo!*" I screamed again, my voice cracking with the effort. The emperor's presence recoiled, then surged forward with renewed fury.

"Fuck off, you dead bastard!" I snarled, mustering everything I had left. "I'm Mercy-fucking-Brown! My body, my choice, you piece of ancient shit!"

One more time, Mercy. Nico's voice was calm, unwavering. *You've got this. I believe in you.*

"*Recedo!*" I screamed, putting every ounce of strength, every bit of defiance, into that one word. The magic flowed from my wand and into my mind. How many times could I pull this off? This ghost wasn't going easy.

Nausea again. Like I'd felt when I was human... before... but this time...

I gagged as the green ghost of the emperor poured out of me with an ear-piercing shriek.

Small victories. We weren't done yet.

A familiar hand grabbed my arm. Too strong. I whipped around to meet Juliet's eyes with mine. It still wasn't her who I saw looking back at me.

"Juliet, don't make me do this," I muttered, hoping against hope that some part of her was still in there. But the ghost puppeteering her body wasn't interested in negotiations.

"*Enerva!*" I shouted, aiming my wand at Juliet's chest. Her eyes went wide with a mix of anger and surprise before she collapsed to the ground, immobilized. Muggs lunged at me next, his movements jerky and unnatural.

"*Enerva!*" I cast again, hitting him squarely in the torso. He crumpled beside Juliet, their bodies twitching as the spell took hold. I didn't know how long it would last, and I wasn't about to stick around to find out.

"Mel!" I gasped, grabbing her by the arm. "We need to get out of here. Now."

"Annabelle, Sebastian, Pauli. And that bald, portly bloke, I forget his name. They're all in the cells," Mel panted, her eyes darting around the throne room like a cornered animal. "The Emperor locked them up when he was running me."

"Then let's grab them and get the hell out of here." I pulled her along as we sprinted down the dark, dank corridors of the underground lair.

"Here!" Mel skidded to a halt in front of a locked steel door. I pressed my hand to the palm reader on the wall. My security clearance still worked. The door popped open. Pauli was slumped against the wall, looking worse for wear but alive.

"Fast! Before the emperor finds a host and can cast his nasty on you again," I urged as I worked the lock.

Pauli groaned as he stood up, rubbing his temples. "I hate that guy! I've never not been able to get it up before, but that guy really makes me go magic flaccid."

"Focus, bitch," I smirked. "Be fabulous and do you."

Pauli grinned. "Oh, honey. I can *always* do fabulous!"

"Brilliant," Mel said. "Annabelle's next door. The hunters are in the third cell on the left."

"Get them out first," I ordered. "Then come for us. And hurry before the emperor gets his mojo back."

"Right!" Pauli's eyes widened as he finally grasped the urgency. In an instant, he shifted into his rainbow-colored boa form and vanished, leaving me and Mel alone in the corridor.

As if on cue, Antoine and Clement, along with a pack of other possessed vamps, rounded the corner. Their eyes glowed with malevolent energy, and they moved with terrifying coordination.

"Shit," I muttered under my breath, raising my wand. "Ready to fight?"

"Always," Mel replied, her fangs bared and eyes blazing.

"Let's dance," I growled, launching myself at the nearest vamp. I knew I was a youngling. I couldn't overpower them the old-fashioned way. But I was still a badass witch. My wand flashed as I cast another *enerva* spell, hitting Clement square in the chest. He staggered back, giving me just enough time to dodge Antoine's attack.

"Mel, behind you!" I shouted, barely avoiding a swipe from one of the other possessed vampires. Mel spun around, delivering a boot to his head.

"Where the hell is Pauli?" I hissed, kicking another vampire away from me. The numbers were overwhelming, and we were running out of time.

Hang on, Mercy! Nico's voice echoed in my mind. *Just a little longer!*

I sighed. "So this is how it's going to be? You there in my head all the time now?"

Is that a problem? Nico asked.

"Who are you talking to?" Mel asked.

"Just fight!" I dodged another attack, this time from one of the possessed orphans. "We only have to last until Pauli gets back!"

"Ask and ye shall receive, bitch!" Pauli's voice rang out cheerfully. Suddenly, the rainbow-colored boa constrictor appeared in a flash of light, wrapping himself around both

Mel and me. His scales shimmered brilliantly, reflecting the surrounding chaos.

"Hold tight, ladies!" Pauli grinned before teleporting us out of there.

The world spun and twisted, colors blurring together until we landed roughly on the streets of Providence. The cold night air hit me like a slap in the face, but it wasn't nearly as jarring as when I was human.

"Now what?" Annabelle asked, her voice shaky but determined. She looked at me, eyes searching for answers. "You're a vampire again?"

I nodded. "But I still have what we need. We still need to find the wizard."

"She's not just any vampire," Mel interjected, a smirk forming on her lips. "I'm your sire now, Mercy."

I scratched the back of my head. "It's true."

Donnie snorted. He clasped his hand over his mouth as if trying to suppress a laugh.

"Just spit it out, Donnie."

He grinned widely. "You're your own vampire grandma!"

"Fuck..."

Then everyone burst into laughter. Annabelle, Sebastian, Mel, and Donnie (of course) was laughing at his own joke. It was weird. There had to be a "you might be a vampire redneck" joke in there somewhere. But we didn't have time for blue collar comedy.

"Alright, alright, laugh it up," I snapped, though I couldn't help but crack a smile myself. "We can crack jokes about my... screwed up lineage later. Right now, we need to find that wizard. We have Mel back, but we still have to save the rest."

"Speaking of which," Mel said, tilting her head as if listening to some distant sound, "I think I know where he is."

"You do?" I asked, hope flaring in my chest.

"Yeah... it's strange," she murmured, her eyes narrowing in concentration. "But that ghost... the energy... it's all connected. And some of it must be lingering in my head."

I patted Mel on the back. "Then lead the way, sire!"

Mel giggled. "Right! Follow me!"

Chapter 17

THE STREETS OF PROVIDENCE were a patchwork of cracked asphalt and flickering streetlights, ghostly under the half-hearted glow of the pre-dawn. We moved like shadows, each step carrying the weight of what lay ahead. Mel led the way, her eyes locked forward with a determination that outshone even the moonlight. The rest of us—Annabelle, Sebastian, Donnie, Pauli, and myself—followed best we could. I had my speed back. I wasn't quite as fast as I used to be, and I needed some blood... badly...

But I kept up. Somehow. Pauli helped the rest of the group keep pace, periodically grabbing them and, in a flash of rainbow light, bringing them to where Mel was leading us.

"Empire Street's just up ahead," Mel whispered. "I think that damn wizard is still there."

When we arrived, I was shocked at the sight. The old Chinatown was a gaping wound in the cityscape, a massive sinkhole that swallowed almost an entire block. At its center stood Anqi Sheng, a figure draped in robes that seemed to ripple with their own dark energy, his eyes glowing with a malevolent light.

He spotted us from a distance. He raised his arms and floated toward us. He screamed something to me in Chinese. Didn't know what it was.

"Sorry we're late," I shouted back. "Traffic was a nightmare."

Before anyone could move, Anqi Sheng raised his hand, and the air crackled with raw magic. A bolt of lightning arced from his fingertips, striking the ground before us and sending a shockwave that knocked us off our feet.

"Son of a—" I gritted out, climbing back to my knees. "I totally expected he'd start monologuing. Bad guys always have shit to say before they try to kill you."

"Ancient Chinese villains," Annabelle muttered. "Not as chatty as the modern American types."

"All I have to do is touch the bastard," I shouted. "I have the power to do the rest. But getting close won't be easy."

"We're on it," Annabelle shouted. She was already moving, her dragon-spirit dagger materializing in her hand. She darted left, circling to flank the wizard. Sebastian followed suit, a giant knife in his hand, as he ducked into a shadow.

"Donnie, cover me!" I shouted, rushing forward. The air shimmered around Anqi Sheng as he summoned a shield, but I aimed for a weak spot—a flicker in the protective barrier. My wand sparked, shooting a stream of concentrated energy at the flicker. It fizzled on impact, barely making a dent.

Anqi Sheng said something in Chinese. Again, couldn't translate it. I'm sure it was something along the lines of "nice try" or "is that all you've got?"

"I've got more where that came from," I sneered. "Enerva!"

He dodged my spell and extended both arms. He spun himself like a tornado in mid-air... then threw the wind he'd built up straight at us. The force threw me backward and into Donnie.

I could swear he copped a feel as we went tumbling to the ground. Or maybe he was just trying *not* to go crashing bald-head first into a nearby car. I decided to assume he was trying to avoid a concussion rather than get a cheap and fleeting thrill *in the middle of a battle* with an ancient wizard. I mean, sure he wouldn't...

Couldn't worry about it at the moment. I sprung to my feet.

"Everyone attack together!" Mel shouted. "He can't stop all of us at once!"

Just then, Sebastian appeared behind the wizard, his dagger poised to strike. The hunter launched himself off a parked car to get the height he needed, but Anqi Sheng whirled around, parrying the blow with a flick of his wrist, sending Sebastian sprawling back to the broken pavement.

Anqi Sheng shook his finger at Sebastian. "Tsk, tsk, tsk!"

"He's too powerful," Sebastian panted, clutching his side. He was in pain, but he forced himself back to his feet.

"Yeah, no shit," I muttered under my breath. "Look everyone! We can't beat him with brute force. And I can't get close enough to him if he sees me coming. I need a distraction!"

"On it!" Annabelle called out. "Pauli, do your thing. When we have the wizard's focus, teleport Mercy straight to him!"

"You got it!" Pauli added.

But as we were formulating our new strategy, Anqi Sheng rose higher into the air, his eyes glowing with malevolent energy. He began raining down spells, bolts of deathly fire magic that exploded on impact, sending chunks of asphalt and dust into the air. The cityscape around us turned into a war zone, the wizard's power turning Providence into a nightmare.

Annabelle launched herself into the air. A pulse of green light—Isabelle was helping out—gave her an extra boost. With Beli in hand, she hurled herself straight at the wizard.

She collided with him, Beli carving a gash in the wizard's stomach. Which he healed with a pulse of golden magic a half-second later. Meanwhile, Donnie went to work with his throwing knives. Hurling one after another at the wizard. I wasn't sure they were reaching him, and it wasn't much of a threat, but it gave us an opening.

"Pauli!" I yelled. "Get me up there! Now! Above him so he doesn't see me coming!"

"Got it, bitch!"

I felt Pauli's rainbow-colored coils wrapping around me. The world blurred for an instant, colors blending and swirling, then solidified again as Pauli released me mid-air, right above Anqi Sheng.

"Good luck, darling!" Pauli called out as I plummeted toward the wizard.

As a human, this would have scared the living daylights out of me. But now? It was just another Tuesday.

I aimed my wand straight at the wizard. His eyes widened in surprise, but before he could react, I crashed into him, jamming the wand into his chest.

"Ever heard of personal space?" I snarled.

"□□□□!" he cursed at me in Chinese, which I didn't understand but definitely got the gist of.

We grappled in mid-air, the wizard's magic keeping us both aloft. He tried to push me away, but I clung to him, my grip like iron. Sparks flew from our point of contact, the force of our combined energies crackling in the air around us.

"You're not getting away that easy," I hissed, tightening my hold.

"☐☐☐☐☐☐☐☐☐?" he spat, his voice filled with contempt.

"Can't understand you, asshole," I gritted out, struggling against his attempts to dislodge me. "But I'm guessing it's something along the lines of 'You'll never stop me,' right?"

He responded by conjuring a gust of wind, trying to throw me off balance. I countered, channeling my own magic through the wand embedded in his chest. We spun through the air, locked in a deadly dance, each trying to gain the upper hand.

"Stubborn, aren't you?" I growled, feeling the strain of maintaining my grip and focus.

"☐☐☐☐☐☐!" he sneered.

"Yeah, yeah, bring it on," I shot back. All I needed was to get a good grip on his head. I was more focused on trying to keep myself up in the air *with* the wizard, since the only way I could was to keep hold of him, than I was getting my spell off.

"Sorry, sweetheart, but it's time for your final curtain call," I whispered through gritted teeth as I finally grabbed his head with both hands. I could feel Nico's power simmering just beneath my skin, ready to be unleashed.

"Now, Nico!" I screamed internally, and the Loa of Balance responded instantly. A surge of energy flowed from me into the wizard. His eyes widened in shock, then horror, as he withered in my grasp.

"□□!" The wizard's voice cracked as his body withered in my hands.

He couldn't hold his magic anymore. Which meant we couldn't stay afloat. We plummeted from the sky, our descent rapid and unforgiving. The ground rushed up to meet us, but I felt no fear.

I was a real vampire girl again.

We hit the earth like a meteor, dirt and debris flying everywhere. I stood up from the crater we'd created, brushing off my clothes. In my hands, the wizard's body was nothing but a lifeless husk, more shriveled than an old raisin left out in the sun.

"Mercy!" Mel shouted, racing towards me with the rest of the team close behind. "You okay?"

"Define 'okay,'" I muttered, dropping the wizard's corpse unceremoniously to the ground. "But yeah, I'm fine."

"Is he...?" Annabelle started, her eyes wide as she looked at the wizard's remains.

"He's done," I confirmed. "But we don't have time to celebrate. The other ghosts could still integrate with the vampires if we don't destroy those statues."

"We only have until sunrise," Mel added, her voice tinged with urgency. "That's what the Emperor kept telling everyone back when he was... inside of me. Ugh, that sounds so dirty when I put it like that."

"Sunrise?" I glanced towards the horizon, and sure enough, the first hints of dawn were starting to appear. "Crap, we're running out of time. We need to get to those terracotta statues buried under all this rubble."

"Move it, people!" Donnie barked, already heading towards the sinkhole where Old Chinatown lay hidden. "We've got work to do!"

"Sun's coming up, Mercy." Mel's voice was somber. "Even with a hundred vampires, we couldn't dig those statues out in time."

"Fuck..." It was the only word appropriate for the moment. And all I could think about was Juliet and Muggs. Mel was right. We didn't have enough time.

Don't give up so fast. Nico's voice reverberated in my mind. *I sucked out more than the wizard's life. I also grabbed his memories. I picked up a few spells I can teach you. Here's one that might work—d"zhèn. It's an earthquake spell."*

"Wait, isn't that what destroyed this place to begin with?"

Trust me.

"Fine," I grumbled, raising my hands towards the rubble. "Everyone, stand back!"

"What's she doing?" Donnie asked, wide-eyed.

"Magic," Sebastian shrugged. "It's what she does."

I took a deep breath and closed my eyes, focusing on the earth beneath me. "D"zhèn," I intoned, feeling the power thrumming through my veins. My wand lay forgotten at my side; I didn't need it anymore. Not for this spell, anyway.

The ground rumbled in response, like a sleeping giant stirring beneath the surface. With a flick of my wrist, boulders began to shift, the earth itself obeying my command. Chunk by chunk, I pulled away the debris, revealing the hidden remnants of Old Chinatown.

"Well, that's new," Annabelle remarked, her eyes wide with awe.

"Yeah, yeah, I'm amazing. Keep your head in the game. Because when I clear a path you need to destroy those damn statues." Sweat beaded on my forehead—not common for a vampire—as I continued to manipulate the earth.

"Mercy, look!" Mel pointed excitedly as I removed a giant slab that hid a chamber *under* the already hidden city we'd been in before. The terracotta statues emerged, their cold, lifeless eyes glowing faintly with an eerie green light.

"That's our target!" I shouted. "No time to lose, people. Let's smash some pottery."

"Go, go, go!" I urged, watching as the team scrambled over the rubble. They spread out, each hunting for statues with a desperate urgency. The sun was rising, casting golden beams across the chaos.

"Mercy, we can't survive this," Mel's voice wavered, her fear palpable. She shielded her eyes from the encroaching sunlight as smoke started simmering on her skin.

"Pauli! Get Mel out of here!" I commanded.

"Mercy!" Mel yelled. "You have to—"

"Got it, bitch!" Pauli wrapped himself around Mel, and with a flash of rainbow light, they vanished.

Mel was right. I had to get out of there, too. But not until I smashed every statue I could get my hands on. Any one of them could be the one responsible for the ghosts inside Juliet or Muggs.

But the sun was already striking my face.

To my surprise, it felt... good. Warm. Comforting. Not the searing agony I had expected.

"You're not burning?" Sebastian's eyebrow was cocked.

I shook my head. "I don't know why not...I should be frying right now."

Surprise.

"Nico." I laughed under my breath as I resumed smashing statues. The rest of the group didn't know about Nico in my head yet. And even if I was alright...we still had to take care of these statues fast. The green light flickering from their eyes was fading fast. "Care to explain?"

"Baron Samedi owed me more than one favor. Let's just say he isn't the one holding onto your soul this time around. I made a few...adjustments to his original design."

I shook my head in disbelief. Niccolo the freaking Amazing! That might work. I couldn't believe it. But I didn't have the time to relish in his magnificence and my surprise.

"*D'zhèn!*" I cast again, feeling the power surge through me. The earth responded eagerly, shifting and cracking as it revealed more of the buried statues.

"Clear the area!" I shouted as the green glow from the statues' eyes were barely flickering now. The ghosts were almost fully integrated with the vampires they possessed.

I raised my hands. A massive chunk of rubble lifted from the ground, hovering above the statues. With a forceful thrust, I brought it down, smashing through the terracotta warriors like they were made of sand.

"Hulk smash!" Donnie laughed.

I shook my head. "Vampire smash. Or maybe…the *Monster Mash!* Get it? See what I did there?"

"Hilarious," Sebastian remarked. But he wasn't laughing. "Now, why the hell aren't you burning? Are you human again?"

Annabelle was looking at me now, also seeking an answer.

I laughed. "Let's just say I have something of a guardian angel. An old friend. And he's full of surprises."

"Do you think we destroyed them all in time?" Annabelle asked.

I shook my head. "Only one way to know. We need to get back to the Underground. Pauli, where'd you take Mel before?"

"Couldn't take her into HQ," Pauli said. "Didn't want to risk her getting taken again by the Emperor. So I dropped her into the sewers."

I nodded. "Good thinking. Go get her and we'll meet back at the Underground. All we can do now is hope."

Chapter 18

The Underground was a chaotic mess of flickering lights and muffled groans. We had just returned from the battle, our bodies bruised but spirits high. The sight of Muggs was enough to melt some of the tension in my shoulders; his serene face amidst the wreckage felt like an anchor.

"Everyone's alive?" I asked, scanning the room for familiar faces. Sebastian gave a tight nod, Annabelle murmured something about protective spells that held. Pauli shifted back into human form, and this time, didn't linger too long in the nude. Annabelle tossed him his clothes, and he slipped them on.

"Where's Juliet?" My voice cracked on the last syllable. I couldn't see her anywhere, and an icy dread crept up my spine.

"She has to be here," Mel said, worry etching lines across her usually composed face. "We smashed all the statues, right? There weren't any more in the rubble..."

I took off running. I dashed through the labyrinthine tunnels, every shadow turning my blood cold. What if I hadn't smashed the right statue in time? What if I had lost Juliet forever? My heart pounded louder than any battle drum. Each step echoed the same fear. Not again. Not another loss.

"Juliet!" I screamed, my voice reverberating off the stone walls. Nothing. Just silence and the scent of damp earth. Panic clawed at my insides. Damn it, where was she?

Just when I thought my heart might explode from the sheer terror, a figure emerged from the darkness. Juliet, looking as nonchalant as ever and dragging a handsome young man behind her. His eyes were glazed, clearly under her thrall.

"Hey Mercy," she called out, waving casually as if she hadn't just put me through emotional hell. Relief flooded through me, and I nearly collapsed.

"Juliet! You scared the deadly daylights out of me!" I enveloped her in a hug.

"Sorry about that. When that ghost that was in me croaked...for good this time...I didn't know how long it would take for you to get back home. And I figured you'd be hungry, so I brought a snack." She gestured to the dazed human beside her.

"He's one of the blood maids who lives down here, you know. Didn't have to go far to get him."

I sighed and shook my head. "I recognize him. Thank you. That was thoughtful. You just had me worried that I didn't save you in time."

"I'm fine!" Juliet laughed. "Call it a date?"

"You sure know how to sweep a girl off her feet."

"Well, I do try," she replied with a wink.

We pulled the human into a nearby room, its dim lighting casting eerie shadows on the walls. The scent of aged wood and dust hung in the air, mingling with the intoxicating aroma of fresh, warm blood. My fangs throbbed as my lips parted.

"Ready?" she asked, her eyes meeting mine.

"Born ready. Or Died ready. Again, I mean."

We bit down simultaneously, our fangs piercing his skin with a satisfying crunch. Blood—rich, warm, and full of life—flooded my mouth. It was like tasting pure ecstasy, each drop fueling a fire within me. But as the crimson liquid flowed, I realized just how insatiable my hunger had become. The more I drank, the harder it was to stop.

"Mercy," Juliet's voice broke through the haze, her hand gripping mine with surprising strength. "Pull away. We don't want to kill the guy."

I fought against the overwhelming urge, forcing myself to release him. The man's pulse slowed, and I licked my lips, savoring the last traces of blood. A sigh escaped me, heavy with frustration.

"Can't believe I'm new again." I wiped my mouth with the back of my hand.

"It doesn't matter," Juliet said, her voice calm but firm. "Nothing's changed."

"Of course, it matters!" I snapped back. "Everything's changed!"

Juliet stared at me blankly. "Why does it matter, Mercy?"

"Because I was the surviving progeny of Niccolo the Damned! The Daughter of the First! Now I'm...well...like Donnie pointed out...I'm my own grandma."

Juliet threw her head back and laughed. "That's a horrible way to put it. But it still doesn't matter."

"How doesn't it matter?" I demanded. "I've lost everything that made me unique, powerful. That lineage was my legacy."

"Do you really think we follow you because of who your vampire daddy was?" Juliet asked, taking my hand in hers. Her grip was steady, grounding. "Please. That has nothing to do with it. We follow you because you're a damn good leader. No matter what shit comes at us, you always find a way forward. You give people hope. That's why you're our queen."

Her words hit me like a punch to the gut. I opened my mouth to argue, but no sound came out. Instead, I found myself looking into her eyes, searching for any sign of insincerity and finding none.

"Hope, huh?"

"Yes, hope," she repeated, squeezing my hand gently. "And your magic kicks ass, too."

"Well, can't deny that," I muttered, a grudging smile tugging at the corners of my lips.

"See? There's the Mercy I know." Juliet winked at me. "Now let's get this place cleaned up and show everyone that their fearless leader is back in action."

"Fearless?" I shook my head. "That's not true, you know. When you were taken like that. Then just a few minutes ago, when I thought I lost you."

Juliet pushed her index finger to my lips. "I know, Mercy. Everyone has *fear*. But you face your fears *every time*. They don't control you. That's what I love about you. Well, one of a dozen or maybe a thousand things I love about you."

"Thanks for saying so. But I don't know," I said, feeling a little lighter but still uncertain. Juliet took my hand and led me back to the throne room.

As we stepped into the room all eyes turned towards us. It was like stepping onto a stage where I hadn't quite memorized my lines yet. Antoine, ever the loyal commander of the Underground vampires, approached with that composed demeanor of his.

"Any orders, my Queen?"

"Do you...do you know what happened to me?" I asked, tilting my head. A part of me dreaded the answer, fearing judgment or pity.

"More or less," he said with a nod, his eyes intense but kind. "What are your orders, my queen?"

Juliet nudged me gently. "Told you so."

"Alright," I said, straightening my posture. "In that case, everyone, let's clean up this place while the sun's out. But tonight...no work. No fight. No battles. I want everyone to go out and have fun. Non-murderous fun, preferably."

"Of course, my queen," Antoine replied. He gave a half-bow, a rare show of formality from him. "As you wish."

"Good," I said. "Now, let's get to work."

I moved through the crowd, exchanging brief words and nods, before spotting Mel in a corner of the throne room, looking both relieved and exhausted.

"Mel," I called out. "Where has everyone gone? Annabelle, Pauli, Sebastian, Donnie?"

"Well..." Mel chuckled. "If you were human...I mean, again...would you want to hang around a bunch of vampires who are trying to get their feet back under them after what happened?"

"Probably not," I admitted with a laugh. "Damn it, though. I didn't even get a chance to say thank you or goodbye."

"They already know it," Mel said, nudging me playfully. "And you can call them anytime. Sebastian and Donnie had to run, though. Sebastian said he had a lead on something that sounded like the monster that took his wife."

My eyes widened. "I should go help him!"

Juliet laughed, the sound both comforting and infuriatingly knowing. "You really think you could find him?"

"Probably not." I shrugged, feeling a mix of frustration and helplessness. "But I can text him, let him know if he needs me..."

"Mercy," Juliet said, her voice softer now as she leaned in and kissed my cheek. "You really don't have to go from one fight to the next. It's okay to *relax* a little."

I sighed, taking a deep breath to steady myself. "But if Sebastian has a lead on his wife...I owe him one!"

"If he wanted help, he'd ask," Juliet pointed out, her tone gentle but firm.

"You're right," I admitted, feeling a knot in my chest loosen just a bit. "Let's get this cleaning done so we can rest up for the night. It's going to be busy come nightfall."

"Busy?" Mel's eyebrow shot up.

"Yes, busy," I repeated, a grin spreading across my face. "We have a dance party to finish. And this time, I'll be damned if anything interrupts our night out."

"Deal," they both chimed in unison, their voices filled with a solidarity that made me believe, just for a moment, that we might actually have a night—one night anyway—without *something* to fight.

The End of Book 8
To Be Continued in *Bloody Fortune*

Want more Sebastian and Donnie? They have their own series! Coming Soon!

Will Sebastian finally find his long-lost wife? Find out! Grab the first three books at theophilusmonroe.com!

Annabelle also has her own series (with Pauli)! Check out THE VOODOO LEGACY!

The VOODOO LEGACY and the entire Recommended Reading Order for Theo's Universe at theophilusmonroe.com

About the Author

Theophilus Monroe is a fantasy author with a knack for real-life characters whose supernatural experiences speak to the pangs of ordinary life. After earning his Ph.D. in Theology, he decided that academic treatises that no one will read (beyond other academics) was a dull way to spend his life. So, he began using his background in religious studies to create new worlds and forms of magic–informed by religious myths, ancient and modern–that would intrigue readers, inspire imaginations, and speak to real-world problems in fantastical ways.

When Theophilus isn't exploring one of his fantasy lands, he is probably playing with one of his three sons, or pumping iron in his home gym, which is currently located in a 40-foot shipping container.

He makes his online home at www.theophilusmonroe.com. He loves answering reader questions—feel free to e-mail him at theophilus@theophilusmonroe.com if the mood strikes you!

Follow on BookBub

Also By Theophilus Monroe

Gates of Eden Universe

In recommended reading order...

The Druid Legacy
Druid's Dance
Bard's Tale
Ovate's Call
Rise of the Morrigan

The Fomorian Wyrmriders
Wyrmrider Ascending
Wyrmrider Vengeance
Wyrmrider Justice
Wyrmrider Academy (Exclusive to Omnibus Edition)

The Voodoo Legacy

Voodoo Academy
Grim Tidings
Death Rites
Watery Graves
Voodoo Queen

The Legacy of a Vampire Witch
Bloody Hell
Bloody Mad
Bloody Wicked
Bloody Devils
Bloody Gods

The Legend of Nyx
Scared Shiftless
Bat Shift Crazy
No Shift, Sherlock
Shift for Brains
Shift Happens
Shift on a Shingle

The Vilokan Asylum of the Magically and Mentally Deranged
The Curse of Cain
The Mark of Cain
Cain and the Cauldron
Cain's Cobras

Crazy Cain
The Wrath of Cain

The Blood Witch Saga
Voodoo and Vampires
Witches and Wolves
Devils and Dragons
Ghouls and Grimoires
Faeries and Fangs
Monsters and Mambos
Wraiths and Warlocks
Shifters and Shenanigans

The Fury of a Vampire Witch
Bloody Queen
Bloody Underground
Bloody Retribution
Bloody Bastards
Bloody Brilliance
Bloody Merry
Bloody Hearts
Bloody Moon
Bloody Fortune
Bloody Rebels
More to come!

The Druid Detective Agency

Merlin's Mantle
Roundtable Nights
Grail of Power
Midsummer Monsters
Stones and Bones
The Wild Hunt
More to come!

Sebastian Winter
Death to All Monsters
Blood Pact
Game Over
More to come!

Other Theophilus Monroe Series

Nanoverse

The Elven Prophecy

Chronicles of Zoey Grimm

The Daywalker Chronicles

Go Ask Your Mother

The Hedge Witch Diaries

AS T.R. MAGNUS

(Epic Fantasy)

Kataklysm
Blightmage
Ember
Radiant
Dreadlord
Deluge

AS JUDAH LAMB

(Christian Thrillers and Supernatural Suspense)

David Shepherd Thrillers (coming soon)

The Unfallen Saga (coming soon)

Printed in Great Britain
by Amazon